"Well, rumour has it she's been engaged twice."

"She broke it off?" Duncan guessed.

Holloway shook his head, looking like the proverbial cat that had gotten in____ cream. "Nope, she didn't have t____ d. She didn't even ge____ nce." Pausing dram____ the count of two ____ left her pregnant."

Because he bel____ extended family that could have easily acquired its own zip code, Duncan's interest went up a notch. "She has kids?"

"Kid," Holloway corrected, holding up his forefinger. "One."

"A daughter. Her name's Melinda. She's almost six. Anything else you want to know?" a melodious low voice coming from directly behind him said, completing the picture.

Duncan turned his chair around a hundred and eighty degrees to face her. Up close the energy almost crackled between them. He would have to be dead not to notice.

CAVANAUGH STRONG

BY
MARIE FERRARELLA

MILLS &
BOON

Published in Great Britain 2014
by Mills & Boon, an imprint of Harlequin (UK) Limited,
Eton House, 18-24 Paradise Road, Richmond, Surrey, TW9 1SR

© 2014 Marie Rydzynski-Ferrarella

ISBN: 978-0-263-91424-5

18-0814

Harlequin (UK) Limited's policy is to use papers that are natural, renewable and recyclable products and made from wood grown in sustainable forests. The logging and manufacturing processes conform to the legal environmental regulations of the country of origin.

Printed and bound in Spain
by Blackprint CPI, Barcelona

Marie Ferrarella, a *USA TODAY* bestselling and RITA® Award-winning author, has written more than two hundred books for Mills & Boon, some under the name Marie Nicole. Her romances are beloved by fans worldwide. Visit her website, www.marieferrarella.com.

To
Patience Bloom,
who lets me spin stories
and
makes my dreams come true

Prologue

"C'mon, Henry, I know you're in there. Did you forget about our lunch date?" Lucinda O'Banyon paused to press her ear against the door she'd just been knocking on, trying to ascertain if she heard any movement within the closed-off room. Though she was well into her seventies, her hearing was still good. "Open up, Henry. I can stand out here longer than you can play possum, old man. You know that."

Lucy took a step back, keeping her eyes on the door.

It remained shut.

Lucy blew out a breath and frowned. This wasn't like Henry.

She and Henry Robbins had an "unofficial" standing date for every other Thursday afternoon for several years now, ever since, in a fit of depression, her friend had sold his house and moved in to the Happy Senior Retirement Home.

As far as Lucy was concerned, the latter was a misnomer if she'd ever heard one.

"There's nothing 'happy' about shoehorning a bunch of older people into tiny rooms and dictating every facet of their lives from here on in," she had told Henry when she'd heard what he planned on doing.

Only a year older than she was, after one surgery had left him feeling weak and far from his old fit self, Henry had been advised by his doctor that he might be better off in a place where help was available 24/7. And even though Lucy had reminded her childhood friend several times that she was only a phone call away, Henry had sold his house and thus opted to "withdraw from life," as she had phrased it.

After she had reconciled herself to his decision, she'd begun visiting him at The Home—and watched, to her horror, Henry become progressively more morose. Which was why she'd made up her mind that today, as tactfully as she could, she was going to suggest that Henry move in with her— strictly on a platonic basis. She intended to make sure he understood that part. They were friends, always had been. It had never gone beyond that.

A year ago, her stipulation would have gotten a wicked response from Henry who fancied himself to be somewhat of a ladies' man. But he'd changed in the past year.

Blessed with incredible health and excellent eyesight, Lucy still had her driver's license at seventy-eight and she made a point of driving Henry as far away as possible from this so-called "happy" home.

He still wasn't opening the door. What was that man up to? she wondered.

"Henry, you leave me no choice. I hope you're decent because I'm coming in," Lucy announced, putting her hand on the doorknob.

"I wouldn't do that," a pleasant, albeit somewhat condescending and authoritative, voice behind her said before she could turn the doorknob and let herself into Henry's room.

Surprised, Lucy turned around to see Amanda Wright. The rather attractive, statuesque dark-haired woman, who volunteered a couple of days a week at the home, was standing almost directly behind her.

"Henry likes his privacy," Amanda told her.

Lucy's back went up. She resented this woman, in her early fifties, presuming to know her lifelong friend better than she did.

For the sake of peace, Lucy took a breath in order to subdue her temper and then said, "Honey, Henry and I go way back. I knew him when he used to smile," she added after a beat.

Amanda raised her chin. Taller by five inches, the woman gave the impression that she was looking down at her. "Henry told me that he wasn't feeling well after breakfast. I suggest that you let him rest," the volunteer told her. "Perhaps even come back later for your little visit."

Lucy had a sudden urge to scratch the woman's eyes out, but she didn't. "And I suggest he tell me so himself," she countered.

She might have been smaller than the younger woman, but Lucy was nothing if not full of sheer grit and determination. She'd come up the hard way and had triumphed over her circumstances. She was not about to allow this woman to dictate to her.

With a deliberate movement, Lucy turned her shoulders around and opened the door.

Fully dressed, appearing to have decided to take a quick nap, Henry was lying very still on his bed.

Too still, Lucy thought, a chill shimmying up and down her spine.

Until just a short time ago, before his surgery had taken place, her friend had been a rather robust and healthy man, especially given his age. However, he had always complained about his inability to sleep. Henry was a light sleeper at best, prone to waking up even if there was the least, inconsequential noise somewhere in the vicinity. That was the reason why she'd gotten him a set of earplugs as a housewarming gift when he had moved into The Home.

"See, he's asleep. You need to leave," Amanda told her, taking her by the arm. The woman looked as if she was ready to hustle her out of Henry's room.

Shrugging out of the woman's hold, Lucy silently

counted to ten in an effort to rein in her temper. She'd had just about enough of this know-it-all woman.

"I'll be the one who decides what I need or don't need to do," Lucy retorted.

Putting her hand on Henry's shoulder, she was about to gently shake her friend awake when she suddenly froze. A coldness swept over her, initiated by the coolness of Henry's skin. She could feel it beneath the thin light blue polo shirt he was wearing.

Fear began to do a soft-shoe through her. She did what she could to block it and the thoughts that were simultaneously being generated.

"Henry," Lucy said, raising her voice. "Wake up. Henry?"

But even as she repeated his name, the sinking feeling inside her chest told her that no amount of calling was going to get her childhood friend to open his eyes.

Henry Robbins was dead.

That made two, she thought numbly.

Chapter 1

"Momma, Lucy's late."

Six-year-old Melinda O'Banyon's knees were sinking into the sofa against the large bay window facing the front walk. The little girl, a miniversion of her mother down to her light red hair, was kneeling there, staring out onto the cul-de-sac street. Having made her announcement, Melinda leaned her forehead against the windowpane and continued to stare out at the semideserted area.

For the moment, no one was leaving or going anywhere.

Detective Noelle O'Banyon pushed thick red bangs out of her eyes and glanced at her watch. It was coming on to eight o'clock in the morning. If she was going to be at the precinct on time, she was going to have to be leaving soon.

Hurry up, Lucy.

"She's not late yet. She has five minutes before she's late," she told her daughter.

Even as she reassured her daughter, a degree of concern slipped in and hovered along the perimeter of her mind. This wasn't like Lucy. Her grandmother wasn't just punctual, she was notoriously early. Always. For the woman to be on time was highly unusual. For her to be late was equal to the Second Coming: it hadn't happened yet.

Noelle felt for her cell phone in her back pocket, debating giving the woman a call. She knew that Lucy would take it as an insult, a silent insinuation that she might have slipped and needed a keeper, but nonetheless, hearing Lucy's voice would ease her mind.

Granted, her feisty, petite grandmother looked and acted not just years but decades younger than she was. Still, the fact of the matter *was* that the woman, who had insisted that Noelle refer to her as "Lucy" rather than any acceptable generic title befitting her station in the scheme of things, such as "Grandma," "Nana" or, God forbid, "Granny," was getting on in years—even if she refused to acknowledge it.

"Lucinda is my given name," her grandmother had revealed, the first time their association took on a more permanent quality. "But you can call me

Lucy. No one else does," she had added by way of making that their own special secret.

Her grandmother was then and continued to be now a live wire, with as much if not more energy as the six-year-old great-granddaughter she currently cared for whenever the need arose. And lately the need arose frequently because Noelle had been promoted to the rank of detective a scant six months ago.

That last development had Noelle thinking of taking another crack at trying to convince her grandmother to give up the apartment she was renting—the one she stayed in only approximately half the time—and just come live with her.

Her last attempt at convincing Lucy had been a failure.

"You'd save money and it'd be easier on you," Noelle had coaxed, thinking the argument more or less made itself.

She'd thought wrong.

"I'm not interested in saving money or 'easier.' I'm interested in my independence," Lucy had responded, cutting the discussion down before it had any time to take root. "I'm the one who taught you about that, remember?" she'd said.

Slipping on her shoes, Noelle glanced over toward her daughter. Melinda was still on the sofa, diligently keeping watch.

C'mon, Lucy, where are you? Noelle thought impatiently.

Though she didn't like to dwell on it, the simple fact was that Lucy *was* in her late seventies and things had a tendency to happen to people at that age.

Lots of things, Noelle thought, biting her lower lip as she carried on a heated internal debate as to whether or not to call her grandmother.

"Whether" won.

Taking out her cell phone, Noelle began to press the series of numbers on the keypad that would successfully connect her to her grandmother's smart phone.

She'd just pressed the last number and was waiting to hear the sound that would tell her the call had gone through when she saw Melinda suddenly jump up and down on the sofa.

"She's here! She's here!" Melinda declared in a triumphant voice.

Scrambling off the sofa, the redheaded pint-size dynamo made an instant beeline for the front door, apparently ready to throw it open.

"Melinda!" Noelle called after her sharply. She managed to stop her daughter in her tracks, just short of yanking open the front door. "What did I tell you about opening the front door?" she asked, crossing the room in a few quick steps.

"Not to," Melinda repeated dutifully, her lower lip sticking out in a pout to end all pouts. "But this is Lucy. We hafta open the door for Lucy," she insisted. "Lucy can't get in unless we open the door."

"Terrific," Noelle muttered under her breath as she shook her head in disbelief. "I'm raising a mini-lawyer." Taking a deep breath, she answered Melinda as if she was talking to an adult instead of a six-year-old. Brighter than most children several years older than she was, Melinda responded to being acknowledged rather than ignored. "Lucy can get in because *I'm* going to open the door for her, not you. When you get to be my size, you can open the door for her, too. Understand?"

The small, open face scrunched up as Melinda obviously pondered her mother's words. "How tall are you, Momma?"

"Taller than you. Look, we'll talk," she promised the little girl, breezing by her. She flipped the lock on her front door to the open position. "Hi!" Noelle said brightly, greeting her grandmother as she walked in.

"Hi," Lucy echoed back in a less-than-enthusiastic tone.

Even if Lucy's tone of voice had sounded chipper, Noelle would have immediately realized that something was definitely wrong. While no one had ever accused Lucinda O'Banyon of being cheerful, she was chipper and behaved closer in age to her great-granddaughter than to the octogenarian she would soon become.

Lucy's voice, coupled with the fact that she had come very close to being late for the first time since Noelle had known the woman, had Noelle back to being concerned. *Really* concerned.

"What's wrong?" she asked the older woman pointedly.

This would have been the place where her still very shapely, attractive and feisty grandmother would have denied that there was anything wrong and then turn the tables on her, putting her on the defensive by demanding to know why she thought anything was wrong, etc.

Noelle knew the way her grandmother responded to events almost as well as she knew how she herself responded to things. Better, actually, since there were times when she was unclear as to her own reactions. She was *never* confused about Lucy's reactions and motivation. Lucy was reliable, predictable and, more than that, the older woman had been her rock for ages now.

Neither one of her parents had ever been very "parental." Her mother, Adriana, viewed being a mother as an inconvenience that got in the way of her lifestyle, and while her father, Howard, had shown signs of wanting some sort of a relationship with his only child, he was firmly entrenched under her mother's thumb. Being so didn't allow him to deviate from the plans Adriana had set in motion for him. He was her escort, her consort and the man who paid for all the expenses despite the fact that in the grand scheme of things, Adriana's family had more money than her father did.

As far back as she could remember, her parents were always going to one country or another, usually getting there via some lavish cruise. That sort of lifestyle had no room for a pubescent daughter who needed regular schooling of some sort. So time and again, her parents would deposit her with her grandmother and take off.

In the beginning, they would pick her up again when they returned from whatever vacation hot spot had lured them away. But by and by, with each trip that became less the case. At first, a few days would go by before they would come for her. But then a few days would knit themselves into a week and then two, until one day, they "forgot" to come for her at all. After that, she stopped seeing her parents between their travels.

Noelle adjusted accordingly.

Though Lucy wasn't ordinarily given to protestations of feelings or any overwhelming displays of emotions, her grandmother made her feelings for her known through actions and the interest that Lucy took in the various events—large or small—occurring in Noelle's life.

Whether it was through her vigilance regarding basic hygiene or making sure that her grades were kept up, her grandmother made a point in having her finger in every pie that was part of her young life.

And Noelle loved her for it.

She noticed now that Lucy was not shrugging off her question, but neither was her grandmother immediately answering it.

Noelle examined the older woman more closely, seeing her grandmother's reluctance to talk coming in direct conflict with an obvious apparent *need* to talk.

Noelle decided to try to help the matter along a little. Her eyes met her grandmother's. "Tell me," she coaxed softly.

Lucy took a deep breath as if bracing herself for the words that were to emerge from her lips. "Henry died," the woman replied quietly.

Henry, Henry. Noelle searched her brain, trying to match the name to a piece of information that might have been carelessly tossed her way in one of their many conversations, both recent and from years past. Lucy was not one to go on at length about anything, but she did mention a great many things in passing.

And then it clicked into place.

"Henry, that's the friend you visit at that senior retirement home on Thursdays," Noelle remembered.

"Every other Thursday," Lucy corrected. "Henry was Dan's friend," her grandmother told her, referring to her late husband, the grandfather she had never known. "And mine," Lucy added in an eerily quiet voice Noelle surmised she was using to camouflage her pain.

Her grandmother and Melinda were the two people she allowed inside the barriers she had built up around herself. Emotions within that limited area came quickly and without restraints.

"Oh, Lucy, I'm so sorry," Noelle cried softly. Stopping short, she knew better than to just go with her instincts without first asking for permission. Generally speaking, Lucy was not a demonstrative person. But this was, after all, an extenuating circumstance. "Is it all right to hug you?"

Lucy nodded, suddenly looking much sadder than she remembered ever seeing her grandmother look. "I think I could use a hug right about now," the older woman said.

Melinda, who had been quietly listening to the exchange, absorbing every word like a short adult-in-training, now took this opportunity to remind her mother and her grandmother of her presence by piping up, "Me, too, Lucy?"

Lucy extended her free hand toward the child, even as she struggled to keep back her hot tears. "You, too, Cupcake."

Melinda instantly pressed her small form against her mother and her grandmother, melting into them and becoming part of the whole.

From a distance, as he watched the woman approaching the squad room where they both worked, Duncan Cavanaugh thought that his almost-brand-new partner looked like a walking tall drink of water. In general, he had always been a man who had never quite satisfied his overwhelming thirst.

But if nothing else, Duncan also had a keen instinct when it came to survival. He just naturally knew when to stand back and when to lean in.

The former was at play here. Newly minted detective Noelle O'Banyon might as well have had a no-trespassing sign taped to her forehead. Tempting though she was and definitely gorgeous, he knew enough to stay back and keep hands off. Even if he hadn't been unexpectedly partnered with her when his former partner Lopez relocated to Miami six months ago to be near his ailing father, Duncan understood that you didn't act on feelings of attraction to someone who clearly had the word *rebuff* written all over her.

At bottom, Duncan had decided that Detective Noelle O'Banyon was his own personal, ongoing trial. A test he could only successfully pass if he was oblivious to her.

Not an easy trick.

Especially when Cameron Holloway, one of the other detectives in Vice, had been quick to give him a heads-up the first time he had learned the name of Lopez's replacement on the Aurora police force.

"Hey, man, this should be very interesting. You're partnered with the Black Widow," the slightly overweight Holloway had gleefully told him.

The unflattering nickname sounded like something an irreverent journalist would slap on an elusive perpetrator, not a label the police would put on one of their own.

"What are you talking about?" Duncan had demanded, confused.

Holloway had looked at him, obviously enjoying the fact that for once he was the one in the know while Duncan was still in the dark.

Grinning broadly, the detective had laughed, "You really don't know, man?"

Duncan enjoyed being challenged. Teased, however, was a different matter and he had little patience with it. Curbing what could be a flash temper on occasions, he replied as coolly as he could, "I wouldn't be asking if I knew."

The other man had smirked, no doubt enjoying the moment and drawing it out for as long as he could. "You ask me, it's nature's way of protecting its own."

"*What* is nature's way of protecting its own?" he'd asked through teeth that were clearly gritted.

Holloway had leaned in, though he still failed to lower his voice. "Well, rumor has it she's been engaged twice."

"Twice," Duncan had echoed while looking at the woman who at that moment was meeting with the head of the vice department, Lieutenant Stewart Jamieson, before being brought out to meet the rest of them.

The grapevine, in the guise of Duncan's older brother, Brennan, had alerted him to the name of his new partner. But Brennan failed to provide certain other pertinent details. If it didn't interest Brennan, he just naturally assumed that it didn't interest anyone else, either.

"She broke it off?" Duncan had guessed.

Holloway had shaken his head, looking like the proverbial cat that had gotten into the cream. "Nope, she didn't have to. They both died. She didn't even get to walk up to the altar once." Pausing dramatically, Holloway had given it to the count of two before adding, "The first one left her pregnant."

Because he belonged to an extended family that could have easily acquired its own zip code, Duncan's interest had gone up a notch. "She has kids?"

"Kid," Holloway had corrected, holding up his forefinger. "One."

"A daughter. Her name's Melinda. She's almost six. Anything else you want to know?" a melodious low voice coming from directly behind him had said, completing the information.

Duncan had turned his chair around a hundred and eighty degrees to face her. Up close the energy had almost crackled between them. He would have had to have been dead not to notice. Just like he would have had to be dead not to notice her delicate, heart-shaped face, her soul-melting green eyes and her flaming red hair. But what got to him most of all was the killer figure that no clothes could adequately hide. He had a feeling that somewhere, in some huge ledger in the sky, he had just been put on notice. His number had finally come up.

Still, he managed to sound unaffected as he calmly asked, "Yeah, where do you buy your shoes, because I didn't hear you come up."

She'd glanced down at her footwear. Not knowing exactly what was expected on her first day in "the big leagues" as Lucy had referred to it, she'd worn her most attractive high heels. Wearing heels always secretly boosted her self-confidence.

"This is just a guess," she'd said drily, "but I don't think that you'd look that good wearing four-inch heels."

"I make it a point never to rule out anything without giving it a fair shot," he'd told her gamely, then rose to his feet as he put out his hand. "Duncan Cavanaugh," he said, introducing himself. "I take it that I'm your new partner."

Jamieson had pointed him out to her, then had to stop to answer a phone call. She'd decided to do the honors herself and dive into her first day here.

"I know," she had replied.

"And your name is?" Duncan had asked, thinking it only polite to pretend that he *didn't* know as much as he did about her—including the information that Holloway had just given him.

Holloway was retreating to his own desk. She had nodded in his direction. "Your friend there didn't tell you?" Noelle had asked.

Duncan remembered grinning. His new partner was quick. He liked that. "He skipped that part."

The two men had appeared to be deep in conversation when she'd approached them. Being the new kid on the block, she'd just assumed that they'd been talking about her. Duncan's answer had made her doubt her assessment. It also made her wonder just *what* they had been discussing. The other man had glanced in her direction three times in that short length of time.

Taking Cavanaugh's hand, she told him, "It's Noelle O'Banyon."

Duncan had nodded as if taking in the information for the first time. "You were born on Christmas?" he'd asked. He couldn't recall hearing a woman called that name before.

"As a matter of fact—no."

It seemed like a logical assumption from where he stood. "Oh."

"I was born on Easter Sunday," she deadpanned.

Duncan had stared at her for a second. He would have wondered if she was putting him on except that she looked so sincere when she'd said that. The woman had to have really out-there parents.

"You're kidding."

She'd laughed, dropping the ruse. "Actually, I am. It was just a name. I'm not even sure if either one of my parents picked it, or if maybe some hospital attendant suggested it."

That had an uncanny sad ring to it. Was she pulling his leg again? He couldn't tell. "Well, either way, it's intriguing."

"If you say so," she'd said.

And so began their dance of words. Over the past six months, they'd each gained a healthy respect for the other's skills and knowledge.

They also got as close as they could as partners

given that one partner held the other at arm's length, Duncan now thought, watching her approach.

But maybe, he concluded as Noelle slid into her seat behind the desk that faced his, that was ultimately all to the good. He'd never had a relationship with a woman that had lasted beyond a month.

Most had had a shorter lifespan. If his interaction with Noelle had gotten serious during off-duty hours, then gone sour, that would, in turn, have laid them both open to absolute *months* of awkwardness.

If not longer.

No, he told himself perhaps a little too firmly for what felt like the umpteenth time, what they had going on between them now was definitely the better way to go.

He ignored the little voice inside his head that whispered, *Sour grapes.*

Chapter 2

"Morning, Sunshine," Duncan quipped.

Noelle raised her eyes to meet his. Given that she had sat down a few minutes ago and she assumed that Cavanaugh had taken note of that as well as seen her enter the squad room, the greeting he'd just offered seemed a little out of place or, at the very least, rather belated.

"What's that supposed to mean?" she asked him.

She watched as her partner's broad shoulders rose and fell in a careless and yet somehow oddly sensual shrug. What the hell was she doing, noticing how broad his shoulders were? What was the matter with her? The size of his shoulders wasn't remotely important here. And yet, she couldn't make herself look away. Couldn't make the strange, tightening feeling in her stomach disappear.

"Nothing," he replied, "just my small attempt to get you to, oh, I don't know, smile maybe?"

That made no sense to her as far as she could see. "By calling me 'Sunshine' or by bringing my attention to the fact that it's morning? Something, by the way, I am well aware of."

The look he gave her was annoyingly knowing. "Get up on the wrong side of the bed again, did we?" Duncan lowered his voice. "Or is your less-than-spectacular mood due to the fact that you woke up to find that it was empty?"

After six months, she'd gotten used to him. Used to the easy, sometimes somewhat annoying banter that meant next to nothing. It was Cavanaugh's way of dealing with boredom and she was okay with that. They all had their little gimmicks.

"It's *always* empty," she emphasized.

"Ah, well, that could be the problem right there," her partner told her as if he'd just made a scientific breakthrough.

Her green eyes narrowed. She was not about to get sucked into discussing her private life, or worse, defending it.

"No, actually, I think the problem is right here, sitting at the desk across from me." The last case they'd been working on had been resolved. If there was a new one in the offing, Cavanaugh would have told her that the second she'd walked in. Obviously they were in between cases. Inactivity made him antsy. "I take it that none of the good citizens of Aurora, California, have given in to the temptation of soliciting anything more lascivious than magazine subscriptions."

Duncan frowned slightly. "Are we talking about hookers?"

"We're talking about the fact that you're bored and having a hard time dealing with it. Maybe one of the other departments is short on manpower. Why don't you make a few inquiries and volunteer your services accordingly?" she suggested.

"And give up sitting across from the ray of sunshine that's known as you?" he asked incredulously. "Not a chance, O'Banyon. Besides, some up-and-coming con artist or identity-theft ring is bound to rear its ugly head all too soon. And, as you've already mentioned, there's always that dependable libido to fall back on."

"Yours or the general public's?" Noelle questioned wryly.

"I plead the Fifth," Duncan said with a grin.

It was the kind of grin that women found sexy and exciting, a grin that went straight to the heart while first stirring the senses and making women—single or otherwise—dream of things that they hadn't even realized they were missing until they had encountered tall, dark and teeth-jarringly handsome Duncan Cavanaugh.

Once upon a time when she'd still been innocent

and naive, Noelle thought, that very same grin would have gotten to her at the speed of light. But after having had her heart broken into countless pieces—so many that she thought it could never be reconstructed to function properly again—and broken not once, but twice, she knew better than to even *think* about attempting to go that treacherous route again. That route was for others who were either more naive or stronger than her to pursue. She had her daughter, her grandmother and her career, and as far as she was now concerned, that was more than enough to fill her world and her time.

"So, how's everything on the home front?" Duncan asked her, changing the subject after several minutes of silence had gone by.

"Peaceful," she answered, then spared him a glance. "Which is more than I can say for here, thanks to present company," she added pointedly.

"Yeah, the squad room is kind of noisy," Duncan agreed, looking around the area while feigning obliviousness to her actual meaning.

He wasn't fooling her. Cavanaugh knew *exactly* what she was talking about, Noelle thought.

"Now might be a very good time to catch up on all those reports that have been piling up," Noelle mentioned.

Duncan rolled his eyes, but he didn't bother commenting on her suggestion. Though he loved his job, loved the idea of carrying on in the family business that was, above all, to serve and protect the people who lived in the same city that he did, documenting that service was a chore that came in only slightly ahead of voluntarily walking into a dentist's office and requesting a root canal be done—for no apparent reason.

Duncan worked his way back to his initial impression of her entrance—and the reason for his previous inquiry. "You were frowning when you came into the squad room just now," he told her.

Noelle deliberately avoided making any eye contact. "Must have been your imagination."

Duncan dropped his playful tone and became serious. "No, and it wasn't my poor vision, either, if that's what you're going to suggest next. You definitely looked like you were disturbed about something just now. Anything I can do?" he offered.

He really was persistent, she'd give him that. She knew that most partners tended to share everything, their histories, their feelings. But that was eventually, and she didn't feel that she was there yet.

For that matter, since she was determined to hold parts of herself in seclusion, she might *never* be in a place where sharing felt comfortable to her. To share was to be vulnerable.

"How about ten seconds of silence?" she asked in response to his offer.

Duncan seemed to seriously consider her request. But his answer, delivered without a smile, still gave him away. "I can do five."

Noelle sighed. *If only.* Out loud she said, "I'll take what I can get."

True to his word, Duncan gave her exactly five seconds, glancing at the second hand on his analog watch, a watch his father had given to him when he'd graduated high school. His father had told him that it had belonged to *his* father and he thought it only fitting that he pass it on.

Ordinarily, Duncan had a fondness for the latest electronic gadgets, but there was something about connecting with his past—a past that had suddenly mushroomed in size around a year ago when he, his siblings and his cousins had discovered that they were part of an already large branch of the Cavanaugh family—that gave him a deep sense of stability as well as intensifying his sense of history.

Counting the seconds now, Duncan looked up at her when the last second faded. "Time's up," he announced.

"How about five more?"

"Maybe later," he answered, then gave her his terms. "After you tell me what's bothering you."

Her eyes locked with his. "You mean other than a partner who won't retreat back into his space and let me work on my reports?"

Duncan inclined his head. "Other than that," he allowed, then reiterated his observation. "You were definitely frowning and you looked preoccupied." He dropped all hint of a bantering tone. "C'mon, give. What's up with you?"

Noelle blew out a breath. "Lucy was pretty upset this morning."

Lucy. *L* before *M*. The alphabetic device was how he remembered who was who. It had taken him a month to get the names straight and stop confusing her grandmother with her daughter.

"Did you find out why?" he asked her.

Noelle nodded. "Henry died."

"Henry." Duncan repeated the name, waiting for some sort of identification to follow it. When his partner wasn't as quick as he felt was prudent, he prodded her a little. "Is that her dog? Or a pet goldfish? Some character on the soap opera that she watches? Or...?"

His voice drifted off as he waited for his partner to set the record straight.

Noelle took offense for her grandmother at the way Duncan had just casually attempted to pigeon-hole a woman she had always felt completely defied any ordinary typecasting. Lucy was and always had been one of a kind.

"She doesn't have a dog or a pet goldfish and the only way that Lucy would wind up watching one of those soap operas would be if someone tied her up in a chair and taped her eyes opened. She absolutely *hates* soap operas," Noelle declared with feeling.

"My mistake. So just who is—or was—Henry?" Duncan asked. "Her boyfriend?" he suddenly guessed.

"Her *friend*," Noelle countered with emphasis.

"According to Lucy, she and Henry had been friends since they were both kids."

Duncan whistled. "Wow, that's a lot of years," he estimated.

"How would you know?" Noelle challenged. "You never met my grandmother."

"Just a calculated guess," he answered, backing off. "So what happened? Did he have a heart attack while they were out, or…?"

Noelle pushed the keyboard back on her desk. So much for catching up. She wasn't going to have any peace until Cavanaugh had the whole story. She had to remember to practice her poker face more often when she was around him.

"They have a standing 'date' every other Thursday— Not like that," she interjected, noting the triumphant look on her partner's face. "They just go out to eat. Anyway, she picks him up every other Thursday to get him out of that depressing senior retirement home he's living in." Since she was stuck telling him this story, she decided to throw in a couple of more details. "Lucy says that ever since Henry moved in there, he's been behaving like a broken man who was just marking time before he died."

Duncan inclined his head. He could see that happening. "Well, technically, we're all just marking time."

Noelle frowned. That was *not* what she wanted to hear. "I'd prefer you keeping your cheery comments to yourself, Cavanaugh," she told him. "Now, do you want me to tell you about this or not?"

He gestured grandly for her to continue with her narrative. "Go ahead."

Noelle banked down her impatience, deciding that Cavanaugh wasn't being deliberately annoying, it just seemed to be something that came naturally to him.

"Anyway, when she got there yesterday and knocked on his door, he didn't answer. After a few minutes, she gave up being polite and just walked in." She could just see her grandmother sailing full steam ahead into the room—and then stopping dead in her tracks once she realized what had happened. Her heart ached for Lucy. "She found him lying on his bed, dead. He was cold," she added, "so he'd probably died a few hours before she got there."

"Had he been ill?" The way Cavanaugh asked the question told her that his interest was clearly piqued. Boredom was really doing a number on the man, she couldn't help thinking.

"No, actually rather amazingly, Henry was in excellent health, especially when you consider that when he'd moved to the retirement home, it was because he'd had surgery and wasn't doing all that well on his own. According to Lucy, his recovery progressed rather slowly. Certainly slower than he was happy about. At the time, he'd needed help doing almost everything. It had to be hard for a proud man like him. But Lucy said he did get better eventually."

"If that's the case, why did he stay at the home?" Duncan asked. "Why didn't he just go back to living in his house?"

"Because it was too late," she answered. "Henry had to sell his house in order to afford living at the retirement home." Her dismissive laugh was totally devoid of any humor. "Those little cramped rooms don't come cheap," she added.

The details surrounding going to live in a retirement home were something he knew nothing about. As far as he could tell, all the older members of his family were still going strong, including Shamus, the family patriarch who had been instrumental in bringing the two factions of the family together.

"How old was he?" Duncan asked.

"Seventy-nine." She waited, expecting Duncan to make a crack about Henry having one foot in the grave or something equally as tasteless—after all, how could someone as vital looking as Duncan even understand what an older person felt? But her partner merely nodded, as if he were taking down information from a witness to a crime. Noelle was pleasantly surprised. Maybe he wasn't so shallow after all.

"So he's a healthy seventy-nine-year-old who just suddenly expires."

"That about covers it all," she agreed, nodding. She'd met Henry a couple of times and had liked the older gentleman, but she couldn't begin to imagine how Lucy had to feel, losing someone who she'd known for so very long. "What makes it worse for

Lucy is that she told me that this is the second person she knew who died in the last six months."

From his perspective, Duncan came to the only logical conclusion that he could. "Is she worried about being next?"

"No!" Noelle cried sharply, then relented, softening her tone as she said, "Well, maybe. What she really is, I think, is lonely. Her circle of friends is growing smaller and I guess it's making her rethink her life."

"Missed opportunities?" he guessed.

But Noelle shook her head. "I don't think so. Lucy never talks about things like opportunities she felt she missed out on. For the most part, she's always been all about the moment, not the past. That was why seeing her like that this morning really kind of threw me."

He completely understood her reaction and it was rather reassuring to know that his partner actually *was* capable of these sorts of feelings. There were times, especially in the beginning, when he'd felt he'd been partnered with a robot or the latest version of someone's rendering of artificial intelligence.

"She's your grandmother, right?" he asked. When Noelle nodded in response, he added, "And you said she raised you."

"She did."

Personally, Duncan couldn't imagine what that had to have been like. Growing up, he'd had both parents around, not to mention the rest of the mob scene.

He was one of seven brothers and sisters, so he'd never had even a moment when he had felt lonely— no matter how much he'd wanted to on more than a couple of occasions.

Duncan got to the crux of his question. "Why do you call her Lucy?"

"Because it's her name," Noelle replied with a straight face. "And because she wouldn't have answered if I'd called her Grandma or Nana or any of those other traditional labels. She once told me that hearing them applied to her would make her feel old. Since she was my whole world—when she didn't have to be—I would have agreed to anything she wanted from me.

"Besides," she went on to say, "it seemed pretty much like a reasonable request to me. Actually, at five, anything an adult asks you to do seems rather reasonable at the time. I never questioned her preference. To be honest, I was so happy to have someone who actually *wanted* to take care of me I would have called her anything she wanted me to call her."

Noelle saw the light that entered her partner's deep green eyes and she quickly headed off what she assumed was his conclusion before he could allow it to grow and flourish.

"My parents didn't abuse me, if that's what you're thinking. They just really didn't notice me very much at all. I was sheltered, fed, clothed and taken in for the necessary shots that eliminated a bunch of childhood diseases—"

Duncan refrained from saying that the same was usually done for a household pet dog. He had no desire to open up any of his partner's old wounds on the outside chance that they might have actually healed. Instead, he said, "But Lucy took more than just a passing interest in you."

Noelle smiled and he noted, not for the first time, that it rather lit up the whole room.

"Exactly," she said. "So I want to be able to be there for her whenever I can." She glanced over toward the small office where Jamieson, their supervisor, was sitting, apparently deeply engrossed in the telephone conversation he was having. "Think Jamieson would mind if I took a couple of hours personal time to attend the funeral with Lucy?" she asked.

For the most part, the lieutenant was an easygoing man. He didn't act as if he had something to prove; neither was he trying to make a reputation on the backs of his detectives.

"I don't see why he would. It's not like we're exactly drowning in work," Duncan pointed out. And then he had another thought—because they weren't drowning in work and because he wanted to meet this woman who preferred having her granddaughter call her by a nickname than the traditional title he personally thought of as endearing. "You want some company?"

The idea seemed to catch Noelle completely off

guard. She looked at him, somewhat confused. "You mean you?"

Duncan laughed at the surprised expression on her face. "Well, I can't very well offer up anyone else's company to you, now can I? I mean, maybe I could—but I wouldn't," he added mischievously. "Yes, O'Banyon, I mean me."

So far the only time she had seen Cavanaugh after hours and out of the office was at Malone's, a local bar that was frequented by members of the Aurora Police Department and that had only been a couple of times. Not to mention by accident because she hadn't known he was going to be there. Up until now, they hadn't made arrangements to meet anywhere that didn't have to do directly with police work.

Since he appeared to be serious—or as serious as he could get—Noelle considered his offer. Cavanaugh was a little unorthodox, but she figured that he meant well and besides, her grandmother responded well to good-looking men. Cavanaugh was nothing if not that.

"Sure," she said. "Why not? If you're there, it might help her keep her chin up." And then she flashed her partner a smile. "Thanks."

"Hey, what's a partner for, right?" he said with an easy, sexy smile.

She tried not to notice just how easily that smile seemed to slip under her skin and unsettle her just before she managed to shut it down.

"Right," she murmured, focusing on the gesture and not on the man. Her life was just about as complicated as she was willing for it to be. There was no room in it for anything extra.

Certainly not for a cocky police detective with magnetic green eyes and a sexy swagger.

Chapter 3

"Are you sure that you're up to this, Lucy?" Noelle asked her grandmother as they approached the cemetery that was on the far side of Aurora's southern boundary three days later.

It was midmorning on Monday. She'd dropped Melinda off at school and driven here for the funeral with Lucy. There was a small, nondenominational chapel on the premises for those who wanted some sort of a service before standing at the deceased's grave site, but her grandmother had opted to bypass that.

Henry never attended a service while he was alive. It'd seem strange having him there now that he was dead, Lucy had reasoned.

"Of course I'm up to this," her grandmother now answered, shortly. "I'm the one who made all the arrangements. It's not like I can call a time-out and put that minister on hold because I'm having heart flutters."

Noelle pulled her car up into the small, uneven parking lot that was in front of the cemetery. Turning off the car's engine, she shifted in her seat to look at her grandmother, searching for any telltale signs that might indicate that Lucy was in any sort of physical distress.

"*Are* you having heart flutters?" Noelle asked, concerned.

"No, I am *not* having heart flutters," Lucinda stated firmly. "Stop looking at me that way, Noely, I'm not some Dresden doll ready to break because you breathed on it. You ought to know that by now." She pressed the release on her seat belt. "Now come on, let's get this over with. Henry's probably looking down right now, annoyed at all the fuss. He never did like making a big deal out of things."

Lucy wasn't fooling her. She knew that her grandmother liked putting on a blustery front, but she was a softy underneath all that. "You sure you don't want to take a minute to take a deep breath or anything?"

"My breathing's just fine, Noely," Lucy assured her. "Besides, if we don't show up soon, the minister's going to think no one's coming and he'll just go and do whatever it is that ministers do when they're not praying over people they didn't know."

Noelle read between the lines. "Are you telling me that no one from the home is going to be coming?"

"That's what I'm telling you. Those old biddies don't like to be reminded that they might be next," Lucy told her loftily.

"How about Henry's family?" Noelle asked, coming around to the passenger side of her car.

As always, her grandmother had already opened the passenger door and gotten out. Lucy wasn't looking for any assistance, but Noelle couldn't help thinking that the woman suddenly appeared rather frail to her right now. But she knew better than to offer her grandmother her arm unless so requested. Lucy was extremely sensitive and proud that way.

She shook her head in response to the question. "Henry didn't have a family. His wife, Jenny, left him years ago, thinking she deserved better—she didn't." Lucy shrugged as if the woman under discussion was of no consequence. "I heard that she died a couple of years back."

"Children? Grandchildren?" Noelle asked, thinking how sad it had to be to know that you didn't have anyone to mourn your passing.

"No and no," Lucy replied, shooting down each question.

Something wasn't adding up for her. "But didn't you say that Henry took out an insurance policy?" she asked. Because it was slightly uphill, progress from the parking lot to the cemetery was slow.

"He did."

Okay, now she was officially confused. "If Henry had no family, just who did he leave his money to?" she asked. And then it dawned on her. Or at least she thought it did. "You?"

Lucy abruptly stopped walking and looked at her incredulously.

"Me?" The woman waved away the very thought. "No. What would I need with Henry's money? It was his friendship I wanted, not his money. Hell, when I came to pick him up on Thursday I was going to talk him into getting out of that depressing place and coming to live with me." They resumed walking as Lucy sighed, resigned. "Guess that's all water under the bridge now, or whatever trite saying fits this occasion. Oh, damn."

They had just walked through the cemetery gates when Lucy stopped short for a second time.

"What's the matter?" Noelle asked, glancing around to see what had caused her grandmother to utter the words of distress.

Lucy remained where she was, her eyes narrowing in obvious displeasure. "She's here."

"She?" Noelle repeated. "Who is 'she'?"

"That annoying volunteer from the retirement home," Lucy said with contempt. "The one who tried to keep me out of his room, acting like she knew Henry better than I did."

Her grandmother had told her all about that when she had recounted all the details surrounding her discovery of Henry's lifeless body. It was obvious to her that Lucy had more than just feelings of friendship cloaked in nostalgia when it came to Henry.

Turning toward the person who had aroused Lucy's anger, she noticed a tall woman, her face all but obscured by the scarf she wore on her head and the dark, oversize sunglasses perched on her nose.

"Want me to arrest her for you, Lucy?" Noelle asked brightly.

Moving forward, Lucy never took her eyes off the woman who'd stirred her ire. "Don't be ridiculous, Noely."

"Sorry. Just want to make you feel better," Noelle told her drily.

Lucy frowned, making no effort to disguise her feelings as she glared across the field at the other woman.

"Besides," she complained, "you don't have anything to charge her with."

Noelle smiled to herself. "You have a point."

And then it was her turn to stop walking, but for an entirely different reason than her grandmother's.

Wearing a dark jacket over his customary black turtleneck and jeans, Duncan Cavanaugh was walking toward them.

She knew he'd said that he'd be there, but she'd thought that, as with everything else, he was just talking. She hadn't really expected the man to actually show up. Especially to a stranger's funeral.

Before she could say anything to let her grandmother know that their party had just increased by one, Lucy's keen radar for good-looking men had alerted her to the tall, broad-shouldered young detective's presence.

Noelle heard her grandmother take in a deep breath, heard the low murmur of appreciation as it fell from her tongue and felt Lucy suddenly straighten up as if an additional twenty to thirty years had just mysteriously melted away. Considering that Lucy already looked a decade younger than she was, that just about made the two of them practically the same age, Noelle judged.

"And whose tasty little morsel is *that?*" Lucy asked under her breath.

The question was a rhetorical one. Consequently she looked at Noelle in utter surprise when she heard her granddaughter inadvertently say, "Mine."

Lucy's eyes widened. And was that a spark of admiration she detected there? Noelle wondered.

"What?"

That had come out all wrong, Noelle thought, upbraiding herself. Why in heaven's name had she said "mine"?

"I mean, I know him," Noelle amended. "He works with me."

At this point, Duncan had seen her and her grandmother and was now striding across the field toward them. He reached them in less than a heartbeat. She'd be the one to know since she was suddenly acutely aware of her own.

"Oh, good, you're here," Duncan said to her with

more than a touch of relief. "I was beginning to think I'd gone to the wrong cemetery or got the time mixed up." And then, very smoothly, Duncan shifted his attention from his stunned-looking partner to the petite woman standing beside her. "You didn't tell me you had a sister, O'Banyon."

"And you didn't tell me your partner failed his vision test," Lucy responded, never tearing her eyes away from what she viewed to be a fine specimen of manhood. "I hope they had the good sense to take away your gun, boy," Lucy told him drolly.

"Feisty," Duncan observed with an approving nod and a wide smile to match. "I see now where Noelle gets it from."

In the six months they'd been together, Noelle had never heard Cavanaugh say her first name. Why the sound of it sent a warm, inviting ripple down her spine made absolutely no sense to her, but now wasn't the time to dwell on it or to ponder why.

"And what is your name?" Lucy asked, her sharp blue eyes pinning the young man in place and devouring every available detail about him. Despite her age, Lucy missed nothing.

"Detective Duncan Cavanaugh, ma'am," he said, giving her his full name.

Deliberately ignoring the fact that Amanda, the volunteer from the home, was making her way toward them to obviously join the tiny circle, Lucy turned so that her attention was strictly on the young man who had just introduced himself.

"Well, not that I don't appreciate the company of a good-looking young man, Duncan Cavanaugh, but just what is it that you are doing here? Have you come to whisk Noelle to the scene of some crime?"

"No, ma'am, I have not. I thought that maybe you and O'Banyon here might like to have some company as you say your final goodbyes." By saying "you and O'Banyon" he really meant the older woman, but he had a feeling that she wouldn't appreciate any references that would make her appear to be vulnerable.

"Oh, you did, did you?" Lucy asked, slanting a glance at her granddaughter before focusing back on the young man before her. "Well, that was very thoughtful of you, Duncan." Glancing around Duncan's muscular frame, Lucy nodded toward the casket that had been set up beside the hole that the grounds-keepers had dug for it the day before. Henry's final resting place. "Right now," she prompted, "I think we'd better get over there before that minister decides to charge me overtime."

Duncan laughed. "Can't have that now, can we?" So saying, Duncan offered his arm to the older woman.

Noelle's eyes met his as she shook her head, trying to warn him off before Lucy's tart tongue told him what he could do with his arm and his assumption as to her frailty.

To her utter amazement, her grandmother not only didn't take off his head, snapping that she was perfectly capable of walking unassisted by some whippersnapper, but Lucy actually slipped her arm through Cavanaugh's and proceeded on to the grave site, blending her footfalls with his.

Or vice versa, Noelle silently amended.

As if reading her mind—not to mention noting her surprise—Duncan glanced over his shoulder at her and smiled broadly.

It was that same half sexy, half enigmatic smile that he'd flashed at her the other day. She had no idea what to make of it, then or now, only that she wished he'd refrain from aiming that smile in her direction. Each time he did, rather than grow progressively more immune to it, she found herself becoming more susceptible to it.

As Lucy, Duncan and she settled in around the perimeter of what was to be Henry's grave, there was no possible way of avoiding the volunteer from the home any longer.

Especially since the woman made a point of taking Lucy's hand and squeezing it as she told her, "I see you made it."

Lucy seemed insulted by the simple, five-word sentence. Venting her displeasure, she looked at the other woman and asked, "What was your first clue?"

"Lucy," Noelle admonished, infusing her grandmother's nickname with a warning note.

To her relief, Lucy looked just the slightest bit contrite. Undoubtedly, it was done strictly because Duncan was present, but she had always made a point of taking what she could get.

Uttering a short laugh, the woman waved a dismissive hand at Lucy's comment. "That's all right. I don't get offended easily."

"Too bad," Lucy commented, keeping her eyes straight ahead and focused on the minister.

The latter took that as his cue to ask, "Will there be any more coming?" He directed his question to the woman who had sought him out on the spur of the moment on Saturday and retained his services for her friend's unexpected demise.

Lucy raised her chin. Noelle's heart quickened when she saw tears shimmering in her grandmother's eyes as she focused on the reason they were actually here.

"Actually, Reverend, this is twice as many people as I thought there'd be," she told him. "Sorry, Henry," she whispered, then looked at the minister and said, "You may start."

The minister nodded and took out a small, worn black book of prayers. Leafing through it, he found the passage he wanted.

The sky above them was a bleak shade of gray, the perfect color for a funeral, as Reverend Edwards recited several brief prayers that seemed rather suited to the occasion.

When he was finished, the minister closed the small book and returned it to the deep pocket he'd kept it in. Scanning the faces of the four people standing on the other side of the grave, he said, "If anyone would like to say something regarding the deceased," he said, glancing from one person to the next, "now would be the time to do it."

Since she had only met Henry once and, to her knowledge, Cavanaugh and Henry had never crossed paths, Noelle thought that the only one who was actually qualified to say something about the recently departed man was Lucy.

Leaning in toward her grandmother, she coaxed her, murmuring, "Go ahead, Lucy."

The next moment she, Duncan and especially Lucy were surprised that Amanda stepped forward, taking the minister up on his invitation.

"I met Henry on my first day as a volunteer at the Happy Senior Retirement Home," the woman began, and in a steady, even cadence, she went on to deliver what could only be described as a eulogy.

A lengthy, rambling eulogy.

Noelle felt her grandmother instantly stiffen beside her and knew that Lucy was struggling to contain her anger and hold her tongue.

She also knew that it was an act of superhuman strength on the part of her grandmother.

The uninvited woman went on and on for several very long minutes, talking about what a loss this was for everyone at the home and how she personally would miss the sound of Henry's voice and his infectious laughter.

Each word she uttered just seemed to stoke Lucy's fury.

The minister was smiling as he appeared to listen, but Noelle had the feeling that the man's smile was forced and that the minister really longed to be somewhere other than at this cemetery, watching a minidrama play itself out.

Noelle could only pray that Lucy would keep herself in check out of respect for Henry as well as for the minister's collar. Lucy could be a real pistol when she wanted to be.

When Amanda finally concluded her eulogy, the minister looked at the remaining attendees at the funeral and asked, "Anyone else want to say anything?"

"Yes," Lucy said between gritted teeth, stepping forward.

Noelle noticed that the minister struggled to suppress a sigh as he gestured for her grandmother to begin.

The smile on Lucy's lips was tight while she looked down at the casket, but Noelle could have sworn she saw her grandmother's lower lip quiver.

"Bet you're glad to be someplace where you don't have to listen to *that* anymore if you don't want to," she told her friend. Patting the casket's lid, she added, "Well, you know I'm going to miss you. That goes without saying. Miss your stubborn arguments, even if I did always manage to talk you out of things." She sighed, struggling to keep her voice from cracking. "Goodbye, Henry. Tell Dan I'll be there in another fifteen years or so. Make sure he behaves himself," she added.

Lucy took a step back and raised her head to look

at the minister. "You can have him lowered into the ground now, Reverend."

With a nod, the minister gazed over their heads and signaled to the two strapping groundskeepers standing off to the side.

Coming forward, the two men went about the business of lowering the casket slowly into the ground. Rather than retreat quickly, despite his apparent desire to do just that, the minister made his way over to Lucy and took her hand in his.

"I know you probably already have one of these cards, but just in case you misplaced it, if you ever feel like you'd like to talk about your friend—or anything at all—I can be reached at this number," he told her.

Lucy closed her hand over the card. "Thank you, Reverend, I appreciate that. But I have been blessed with a granddaughter who actually listens."

The minister glanced at Noelle and then at the young man standing on the older woman's other side. He smiled in understanding.

"Not everyone is that lucky. You are a very fortunate woman, Mrs. O'Banyon," he told her. "In many ways. But I think you already know that." The minister looked at Noelle and then at Duncan. "And you have a very nice family."

With that, the minister took his leave.

Even as he began walking away, the man's words registered belatedly with Noelle. She immediately opened her mouth to set him straight and correct the misconception that the minister had obviously managed to make. She realized that the man thought she and Duncan were married.

Raising her voice, she called after the minister, "Oh, but he's not—"

"Save it, Noely," her grandmother advised. "The reverend's out of earshot—and it doesn't matter anyway," Lucy said.

It was time to go. She'd said what she wanted to say, paid her respects to a lifelong friend as well as paid for his funeral. There was nothing more to be done here. Turning to Duncan, Lucy said, "Young man, your arm, please."

For the second time in a very short span, Noelle's mouth dropped open again. If she didn't know better, she would have said her grandmother was flirting with Cavanaugh.

Keeping the observation to herself, she fell into step behind her grandmother and her partner. Lucy seemed to be hanging on his every word, not to mention physically hanging on his arm as she allowed him to guide her back to the car.

The end of the world, Noelle decided, was undoubtedly being announced sometime in the next few hours.

Chapter 4

It kept nagging at her, even as she sat at her desk at work.

Noelle knew she had a great many things—small and large—to occupy her mind, not the least of which was the pile of reports she'd had to catch up on during the lull the division was currently experiencing. She had no reason to dwell, especially after two weeks, on a small, seemingly throwaway detail about Lucy's deceased friend. Lucy had only mentioned it in passing while talking about the general state of Henry's health.

After all, Lucy hadn't indicated that she was in any way bothered by the existence of this fact.

But she was.

Especially since she hadn't gotten a good answer to her question from Lucy when she'd asked about this loose detail.

"Okay, what are you chewing on?" Duncan asked her.

The question caught her off guard. As far as she knew, she'd given no indication that something was bothering her. Maybe she needed to work on her poker face a little, she thought.

"What?" It had taken her a moment to hear Cavanaugh's question, almost as if her brain was on some sort of five-second delay. Hearing the inquiry, she shook her head. "Oh, nothing," she said, hoping that was the end of it.

It wasn't. She should have known better. This was Cavanaugh, a man who managed to take "annoying" and turn it into an art form. Even his good looks managed to annoy her. Annoy her because she couldn't seem to get to the point where she could just ignore them, or become oblivious to them. If anything, the man continued to increasingly disturb her peace.

"Don't give me that. I've been your partner for six months and I've gotten to know that face," Duncan told her. "Something's bugging you and it's been bugging you for a while now."

Rather than tell him what she was thinking about, she switched subjects, taking the opportunity to clear up something else. "Okay, if you must know, I'm just trying to figure out what your angle is." She saw a hint of confusion furrow his brow, so she elaborated. "Why did you go out of your way to attend a funeral for someone you didn't know?"

"Because you were going and it's what partners do for each other," he replied. "But that's not it," he added. It was her turn to look quizzical and his turn to clarify his point. "That's not what's making you chew on your lower lip. That's your tell, you know. That's what you do when you're trying to work something out in your head. Now, what is it?" he asked. "I think you should tell me before you wind up chewing right through your lip."

Noelle didn't like sharing things until she had a handle on it. In this case, she had no answer, nothing that stood out for her as even a *remote* answer, much less a reasonable one.

But if Cavanaugh knew her, she also knew him. He would continue badgering her, most likely at inopportune times, until she gave him an acceptable answer to his question.

She might as well save herself some grief and aggravation and tell him. "I'm trying to figure out why a man who had no family and only one really dedicated friend would take out an insurance policy. Henry had to have had something better to spend his money on than an insurance premium, don't you think?"

Duncan shrugged. "Depends. Who got the money once Henry was gone?"

Noelle sighed, frustrated. "I asked my grandmother that, but she got sidetracked before she could give me an answer."

"It's been a couple of weeks. She's had a little time to deal with the loss. Ask her now if it's bothering you that much," he suggested. And then Duncan paused, studying her for a prolonged moment as a thought hit him. "You don't think that Henry died of natural causes, do you?" he guessed.

Noelle pressed her lips together. She still wasn't in control of this subject and she didn't want to say things that put her in a vulnerable position. Devoid of vanity, she still liked being perceived as generally being on top of things, not someone who allowed their imagination to run wild.

"Lucy said he was the picture of health," she replied cautiously.

"The problem with pictures is that you only see what's on the surface. There could be things going on underneath that you have no idea about. Old people die. It's what's expected, what they do. Nobody lives forever, O'Banyon."

"Right," she said, blowing out a frustrated breath. "It's what's expected," she repeated. And that could just be the whole point, she realized. "So nobody thinks twice, nobody looks into it if an old man like Henry suddenly dies." Impassioned, Noelle leaned forward, lowering her voice so that only Cavanaugh heard her. "What if Henry *was* in the pink of health? What if someone decided to 'help' him along?" she postulated. She knew how crazy this sounded—but he had asked. "What if someone killed Henry before his time?"

"You mean like a mercy killing?"

"Mercy killing usually involves terminal patients who are suffering. Lucy said that Henry wasn't sick," she reminded him.

"If you feel that way, that your grandmother's friend was murdered, why don't you bring this to Homicide's attention?" he asked.

For a smart cop, he was missing the obvious, Noelle thought. "And get labeled as a troublemaker? I don't think so." She was cautious, even if she did explore all the options. "I need some kind of tangible proof before I say anything to anyone."

"If you want, I could bring it to Brennan's attention," he said, mentioning his older brother who was currently a detective in the department's homicide division. "He owes me a favor—or two," Duncan told her, thinking of an off-the-record surveillance detail he'd performed for his brother recently. That had ultimately brought down a notorious flesh trafficker and was still fresh in Brennan's mind.

"Why would you do that?" Noelle had never liked being in anyone's debt. Her eyes narrowed suspiciously as she looked at him.

"Because it's obviously bothering you," Duncan answered, then asked a question of his own. "Have you always been this suspicious, or do I rate some kind of special treatment?"

Both, she thought. Out loud she said, "Let's just say that I like being careful. A lot of people have disappointed me."

Her answer made him wonder things about her that couldn't be answered in a sentence or two. Still waters really did run deep.

"I'm not 'a lot of people,'" Duncan pointed out.

No, he certainly wasn't. Not with those looks, she thought. And it was precisely those looks that had put her on high alert and her guard up.

"I like to find things out for myself," Noelle replied.

"The only way I see that happening is if I wind up doing what I say I'm going to do—hand this over to Brennan—with no ulterior motive," he added, thinking that might have occurred to her next.

"I'm probably making a mountain out of a molehill."

"Possibly," Duncan agreed. "But then again," he went on quickly, before his partner could shut down the discussion, "you could be reacting to a gut feeling and in my opinion, gut feelings trump a great deal of schooling and logic." He looked at her pointedly. "You can't teach 'gut feelings.' It's just something you have to be opened to."

"Wait, let me guess. Police Work 101?"

He let the crack slide and gave her a serious answer. "More like a Cavanaugh credo."

For a second she'd forgotten that he came from a

family that had more cops than most small towns. Taking a deep breath, Noelle lightened up.

"I appreciate your support," she told him and realized that she actually did. "But I'd like to 'chew on this,' as you called it, for a while before I ask you to follow through on it." Because there might not be anything to all this, she didn't want to really get him involved until she was sure.

He shrugged. "Suit yourself," he answered, adding, "Do what you have to do and then, if you feel that there's anything there, get back to me. My offer to help you is still on the table."

She nodded, mentally withdrawing from the conversation. But just before she did, she glanced up at him and said, "Cavanaugh?"

He raised an eyebrow. "Yeah?"

She inclined her head, as if she was almost embarrassed to say it, then murmured, "Thanks."

His grin was lopsided and she tried not to look at it for more than a single beat, because it did things to her, sparked a new kind of awareness.

"Don't mention it," Duncan said.

She probably would have been better off if she hadn't, Noelle thought. That she had tendered her thanks left her open to his speculation and she didn't like being pigeonholed.

Noelle bided her time. She waited until her partner finally took a trip to the vending machine to secure a little energy wrapped in silver foil a couple of hours later.

The minute Cavanaugh was clear of the squad room, she pushed aside the files she'd been inputting and called her grandmother.

The woman picked up her phone on the second ring. "Hello?"

"Lucy, it's me, Noelle. How are you doing?" she asked, wanting to check on her grandmother's state of mind before she asked her anything else.

"Fine, sweetheart. Life goes on, right?" Lucy asked with a note of cheerfulness. "Don't worry about me."

"Comes with the territory, remember?" Noelle asked. "You taught me that." And then she got down to the main reason for her call. "Listen, Lucy, remember when you told me about how healthy Henry was and that he'd gotten himself a life insurance policy?"

"Yes?"

She could hear the patient wariness in Lucy's voice, as if her grandmother was waiting for a shoe to fall. "I asked you who he left his money to and you never got around to telling me."

Lucy laughed shortly. "There's a reason for that," she anwered. "I don't know. He never told me."

"You didn't ask?" Noelle asked incredulously. Was everyone devoid of curiosity? Or did she just have a double dose of it?

She was surprised by her grandmother's tone. "I had more important things on my mind than asking questions about such foolishness."

Noelle wasn't ready to give up just yet. "Didn't it strike you as odd that he'd do something like that at his age?"

Lucy laughed again, this time there was no edge to the sound, only a flash of irony. "Honey, there were a lot of odd things about Henry." And then she asked, "What are you getting at?"

Noelle wasn't ready to voice her suspicions just yet. Lucy had been through enough for the moment. She didn't want to add the possibility of her friend being murdered for the insurance money until she was absolutely sure of it. If it turned out to be a wild theory, there was no point in getting Lucy upset.

"I'm just filling out the picture for myself," she told her grandmother.

Lucy was sharp enough to quickly put the pieces together. "You don't think that Henry died of natural causes, do you?"

"I didn't say that," Noelle tactfully pointed out.

"You didn't have to," Lucy said. "I can hear it in your voice. To be honest, if I had to make a choice, I would have said that Sally was the one who didn't die of natural causes."

"Sally?" Noelle echoed.

"That other person I was referring to when I told

you that Henry was the second friend I had who'd died in the last few months," she explained to Noelle.

Her grandmother hadn't really said anything much about this first friend who had died. Or maybe she hadn't really been paying attention. It could have happened when she and Cavanaugh were hip-deep in getting the goods on a designer-handbag counterfeiting ring.

"Tell me about Sally," she coaxed.

There was a lengthy pause on the other end. She was just about to ask if Lucy had heard her when the other woman began to answer. "There isn't all that much to tell, really. One day she seemed like she was in fantastic shape—training for a 5 km marathon—the next day, she was gone."

"Dead?" Noelle asked.

"Very. Her running partner got concerned when she didn't show up in the park for their daily run, so she went to Sally's house—Sally had given her a key. She let herself in when there was no answer and she found Sally in her bed, unresponsive and very cold. It looked like she'd died somewhere in the middle of the night."

"And you were suspicious?" Noelle pressed, wanting to get to the bottom line.

"Well, yes. Sally said she'd gotten a clean bill of health from her doctor when she went for a checkup a couple of months earlier—that was just before she applied for a life insurance policy."

Noelle's antennae went up on high alert. Two life insurance policies on senior citizens, two deaths. *Was* there a pattern here?

Out of the corner of her eye, she saw Cavanaugh returning to his desk. His attention was clearly on her and her end of the conversation. She thought of calling her grandmother back. But right now, getting more details out of Lucy was more important to her than not arousing her partner's radar.

"Then Sally had applied for insurance, too?" she asked, just to double-check her facts.

"Yes."

That couldn't be just a coincidence, could it? That had to be a connection. Now all she needed was the right follow-through. "Why didn't you tell me about Sally? *And* her life insurance policy?" she added for emphasis.

Lucy made no apologies for her actions—or her lack of them. "Well, to be honest, I didn't think you'd be interested."

Now came the big question. Mentally, Noelle crossed her fingers. "Would you happen to know if Sally got her life insurance policy through the same company that Henry did?"

Lucy paused for a moment, obviously thinking and trying to remember the answer to the question. "I think she'd said something about deciding to go through a broker. Supposedly the broker was going to turn her onto the best insurance company to go with."

"Do you have his name?"

"Her," Lucy corrected. "I remember Sally said her broker was a woman and that she found women easier to deal with than men."

Noelle saw Duncan eyeing her curiously. For once it looked as if he wasn't having any luck piecing together what was going on. Good.

"Yes, I know what she means," she told her grandmother. "Do you remember the broker's name?" she asked hopefully.

The next second, her heart sank—then buoyed up again, all in the space of one sentence.

"No, but I have a card here somewhere. Sally gave me the woman's card, saying that I might want to get a life insurance policy so that you won't have to face any unexpected expenses that might come up when it's my turn to kick the bucket."

The last thing in the world Noelle wanted to think of was her grandmother's passing. "You're not going to be kicking any buckets any time soon," she informed the other woman firmly.

The laugh was short, humorless and ironic. "That's what I told Sally, but to humor her, I took the card anyway."

It was a good thing that she had. It might lead them to something—or at least allow them to rule out something if they didn't.

"Do me a favor, Lucy," she went on to tell her grandmother. "When you go pick up Melinda from school today, could you swing by your place and find that card for me?"

"Then you *do* think something's wrong, don't you?" Lucy pressed.

As far as the world was concerned, she processed everything slowly. It was only the brass—and her partner—who knew exactly how fast she could be if necessary. And she intended to keep it that way.

"Not sure yet, but having all the facts won't hurt," she answered her grandmother evasively.

She heard her grandmother snort on the other end and knew that the woman wasn't buying that. "I'm not sure where I put the woman's card, but I'll give you a call as soon as I find it."

"Great." She was about to hang up when she remembered something else. "Oh, wait, one more question, Lucy. Did Sally have a family?"

Lucy thought for a second, wanting to make sure she had her facts straight. "A few distant second cousins somewhere," she recalled, "but beyond that, I don't think so."

"She was never married?"

"No, poor thing. According to her, she never found Mr. Right. I tried to talk her into Mr. Right Now, but Sally was stubborn. She didn't want to hear about it. She said that she wanted the bells and the banjos—or nothing. She settled for nothing."

Well, she couldn't blame Sally for wanting it all, Noelle thought. On the pragmatic side, this was beginning to sound eerily like a pattern that led to a fatal end.

"Do you know who *she* took the policy out for?" Noelle asked next.

"I think she mentioned that it was some charity or foundation. Sally was into helping others whenever she could. I told her to spend the premium money on herself, that you only go around once in life and should enjoy yourself, but she was adamant. Said that someone told her it was a good thing she was doing."

Noelle could feel the hairs on the back of her neck standing up. Was this "someone" the person who was responsible for her friend's death? Possibly even for Henry's death? She knew that sounded far-fetched and pretty much off-the-wall, but you never knew when something would pay off—and truth had a habit of being a lot stranger than fiction.

"Would you happen to know who this 'someone' was?" she asked.

"Haven't a clue. I'd better go," Lucy said abruptly. "School's letting out soon. I'll give you a call when and if I find the card," she promised. The next moment, the line went dead.

As Noelle hung up her desk phone, she could almost *feel* Cavanaugh watching her. When she raised her head so that her eyes met his, he had one question for her.

"What did I miss?"

She tried to play dumb, hoping to get him to drop the subject. "What do you mean?"

He laughed, not taken in for a second. "I mean that I could see your detective antennae go up and quiver clear across the room and all the way down the hall. Now stop playing innocent and come clean. What did I miss?" he repeated.

Chapter 5

"**Y**ou didn't miss anything," Noelle replied in a deliberately calm, disinterested voice, hoping that would be the end of it. But when Duncan continued looking at her, she knew he expected more. "I was just talking to Lucy."

"I gathered that much. And…?" he prompted, waiting.

Why couldn't she have gotten a partner who knew how to back off and mind his own business? she wondered. "And nothing."

"Your grandmother just called to hear the sound of your voice?" he asked.

He wasn't being entirely sarcastic since he knew that there was an outside chance that Noelle's grandmother had just wanted to touch base, to hear the sound of her granddaughter's voice as a way of dealing with her grief over losing a lifelong friend. He was the first to acknowledge that the familiar offered some comfort.

But he had a gut feeling that there was more to the call than that. Pressing Noelle a little on the subject couldn't hurt.

"She didn't call me."

"Ah."

Noelle narrowed her eyes, annoyed at the sound. Annoyed that he had managed to get into her head. "I called to see how she was doing."

Duncan inclined his head as if to coax her along. "And?"

After a moment, she finally surrendered. "And to ask if she knew who Henry left his money to."

"I meant 'and what did she say' when you asked how she was doing, but let's go with this instead," he urged, pleased that she had volunteered something. "*Did* she know who he left his money to?"

"No, she didn't know," Noelle admitted. "She did say that her other friend left her insurance money to some charitable foundation."

This was obviously taking a whole new turn. "Wait, what?" he asked, unclear as to what she was telling him. "That other friend you told me your grandmother lost, he was insured, too?"

"She," Noelle corrected.

Duncan backtracked a step to get back on point. "*She* was insured, too?"

Okay, so he *hadn't* figured it out and she'd given Cavanaugh credit where it wasn't due. Next time, she was going to have to listen more carefully to what he was actually saying before inadvertently volunteering information.

With a sigh, she answered, "Yes."

"And, let me guess, the woman had no family, either?"

"No family," she confirmed. "At least, none that Lucy knew about. My grandmother also said that her friend Sally was in top condition. The woman ran five miles daily. According to Lucy, she was some sort of phenomenon and was always training for marathons."

"Lots of people train for marathons."

Noelle realized he was missing the salient point. "Yes, I know, but according to Lucy her friend was in her eighties."

She saw a flittering of surprise pass over his face. Was it her imagination, or did that somehow emphasize his cheekbones, giving him an almost brooding-romantic look.

Oh c'mon now, Noely, get a grip. You're staring down a possible double homicide and all you can do is get dreamy-eyed over his cheekbones? Are you having some sort of a crisis here? she demanded of herself.

"Now *that's* unusual," Duncan commented. "What did she die of?"

"Lucy said that her running partner found her in her bed, dead. Lucy didn't say it specifically, but I think they just assumed it was a heart attack."

"Did anyone do an autopsy?"

"Not that Lucy mentioned." She had a feeling that the coroner had just gone with the obvious. After all, heart attacks were a common cause of death for people in their eighties. "Maybe we should find out," she suggested.

"Homicide isn't our purview, remember?"

Noelle paused for a second, then rolled her eyes and said, "I know. What was I thinking?"

There was only a hint of a smile on Duncan's lips as he shook his head and said, "Uh-uh."

"Uh-uh?" she echoed back at him.

"Not buying it," he elaborated. "You're giving up too easy."

"Just bowing to your superior wisdom," she told him tongue in cheek.

"Now I really *am* suspicious," he said as he looked at her knowingly. "You're going to investigate on your own, aren't you?"

They'd been partners for less than a year. Maybe the boundaries needed to be refreshed, since he'd seemed to have forgotten them. "What I do on my own time, Cavanaugh, is my own business."

"That's true," he agreed. "*If* you're talking about indulging in adopting pet snakes or living in sweats on your day off. But not if what you're doing on your time off involves dead bodies."

She couldn't really deny it vehemently because she'd always been unable to lie outright. All she could do was allude to a denial. "Like you said, homicide isn't our purview."

"There are a lot of other angles at play here," Duncan said as he rolled the matter over in his head, thinking out loud. "Insurance fraud might be behind this—*if* these people were killed strictly to collect on their policies." And fraud *was* something they could definitely investigate. "We need to find out what insurance company was involved, who wrote the policies and which so-called charitable foundation or foundations collected once the generous donor stopped breathing."

She looked at him with new respect. "You really think we can get the green light to investigate this as insurance fraud?"

"The only way to find out is to ask. We have a fifty-fifty chance of getting an okay."

She glanced toward Jamieson's glass office. "But if the lieutenant says no, that'll officially shut us down—isn't it better to ask forgiveness than permission?" she asked, remembering having heard the old saying somewhere once.

He laughed. Those were his feelings. He hadn't thought that they'd be hers. Maybe she wasn't as straitlaced as he'd thought. "You've got more going on under those bangs than I thought. Tell you what, why don't we do a little investigating off the record first to see what we can come up with."

"Where do you want to begin?" she asked, getting up and reaching for her jacket.

"With Brenda," he told her, then nodded at the jacket. "You won't need that." With that, he led the way out of the squad room.

Noelle was quick to follow him out and catch up. "Brenda?" she questioned.

"Brenda Cavanaugh. She's the head of the tech lab."

Another Cavanaugh. She should have known, Noelle thought as they approached the bank of elevators. "You people have a Cavanaugh for everything, don't you? Is she your sister?"

He grinned at her first comment. He supposed it might seem that way to some people. There certainly were enough of them throughout the police department. That worked both for them as well as against them at times. "She's the chief of d's daughter-in-law. I'm told she works magic on that computer of hers."

"Magic is good," Noelle agreed as the elevator arrived. She preceded him. Her partner pressed the button for the basement. "But won't she balk at being asked to do something unofficial?"

"From what I hear," he answered, "Brenda knows that over half of good police work is done by flying by the seat of your pants."

"From what you hear," Noelle repeated. She was

getting a very uneasy feeling about this. "Does that mean you haven't dealt with her yourself?"

"Not until today." He saw the hesitation in Noelle's eyes as the elevator brought them down to the basement and the doors opened. "But I have met her and she's very approachable," he was quick to reassure.

"Where did you meet her?" she asked.

"At Andrew's house." Realizing that since his partner hadn't known who Brenda was, she might also not know who he was referring to when he said Andrew. Duncan added, "Andrew's the former chief of police. He's got a thing for family gatherings and likes to throw parties to bring as many of us together as he can." The next moment, a thought struck him as he led the way through the maze that would eventually bring them to the tech lab. "You should come the next time he has one," he invited. "And bring your grandmother."

"Just like that," Noelle scoffed.

To her surprise, he didn't back off. "Sure. The more the merrier, Andrew's always saying."

He had to be kidding, right? "I should just pop up at the former chief of police's house with Lucy some weekend."

"Word has it that everybody else does," he assured her.

How gullible did he think she was? She didn't crash parties. "You said they were *family* gatherings. I'm not family," she pointed out.

"You're a cop, that makes you family." Duncan saw the skepticism in her eyes. "Hey, that's not my philosophy, that's Andrew's," he informed her, then added, "And it might help your grandmother get her mind off her friends dying."

Noelle was not about to accept pity for her grandmother. "Lucy's a rock," she said defensively.

"No, she's not," he countered, then quickly said, "Rocks don't have friends," before she could launch into a rebuttal.

Caught off guard by the flippant remark, she was at a loss to respond. The next second, she had collided into him because Duncan had abruptly stopped walking.

If he noticed how soft her contours felt against him, he gave no indication. Instead, he merely said, "We're here."

Pausing to deliver a single, quick rap against the closed door, he opened it and gestured for Noelle to walk in first.

When she did, Noelle quickly looked around the newly refurbished tech lab. There were several people within the lab, their attention completely focused on the state-of-the-art computers that were on their desks. The technicians' backs were all turned to the door.

Brenda Cavanaugh's desk was twice as large as her staff's. That was because she had two computers hooked up to two separate monitors on it.

Her desk also faced the door so that she was able to see everyone who came in.

What began as a quick, ascertaining glance as the duo entered turned into a gaze as partial recognition set in. Brenda's fingers, however, never stopped for even an instant. They continued flying across the keyboard.

Duncan led the way to Brenda's desk. Not expecting her to recognize him, he waited until he reached it before introducing himself. "Brenda, I'm—"

She didn't bother to let him finish. "I know who you are, Duncan," she told him. "I'm good with names and faces. Given the family I married into, I have to be," she added, flashing a warm smile at Noelle. "But yours I don't know," she confessed, looking at Duncan's partner.

Noelle was quick to enlighten her. "I'm Noelle O'Banyon."

"Your partner?" Brenda asked, her eyes shifting to Duncan.

"Yes and indirectly, kind of the reason we're here," he told Brenda.

"I'm listening," Brenda said.

As succinctly as possible, Duncan summarized why they'd come down to the lab to see her. He made sure to emphasize the oddity of both deceased senior citizens having been signed up for insurance policies within the past eighteen months despite not having any relatives or significant others in their lives to appoint as their beneficiaries.

"And now you'd like…?" Brenda's voice trailed off as she left her question open-ended.

"As much information about both deceased people as possible," Noelle told the head of the lab before Duncan could answer. "We need to know what insurance company underwrote the policies, what agent sold the polices and most important, the name of the so-called nonprofit foundations that were on the receiving end of the death benefits."

Brenda nodded, taking it all in. "In other words, pretty much everything to do with these policies."

"Pretty much," Duncan echoed.

Brenda was silent for a moment, thinking. "You believe these two people were set up," she concluded.

"Well, at the very least, we'd like to rule that out," Duncan answered.

"Diplomatic save," Brenda replied, inclining her head. "Is this an undercover operation?" she asked.

Duncan wanted to give her plausible deniability in case this somehow either blew up in their faces or came back to bite them. Just because something about the case *felt* off didn't necessarily mean that it actually was—in which case they would be doing a great deal of unnecessary work.

"Let's just say it's off-the-record," he answered.

"How off?" Brenda asked.

Cavanaugh was right. The lady was sharp. Noelle decided that it was in their best interest to tell the woman the truth, with no reservations.

"The two people we need you to investigate were

my grandmother's friends. When she told me about their sudden deaths, then mentioned that each had recently signed up for a life insurance policy, the whole thing seemed rather suspicious to me."

Brenda extrapolated on the statement she'd just been given. "You think someone's getting old people to apply for life insurance and then killing them so the policy could pay out."

Noelle inclined her head. It sounded so much worse when Brenda put it into words. "Something like that, yes," Noelle admitted.

"So you think your grandmother might be next?"

Noelle's jaw dropped open. Where had Brenda gotten that idea from? Of course, now that the thought had been planted, she wouldn't be able to focus on anything else.

"Oh, no, not her," Noelle denied adamantly. "Lucy's too smart to be taken in by that kind of thing—and besides, we're her family."

"'We'?" Brenda asked, immediately picking up on the pronoun.

"My daughter and I," Noelle explained. "The people who were killed had no family. I think the killer or killers knew that before they set them each up."

"Makes it easier," Brenda commented. "There's no one to contest the insurance policy's allocation of death-benefit money," she concluded. The next moment, she was nodding at them. "Okay. I'll get to this—" she gestured at the notes she'd taken "—as soon as I can. I'm afraid that I've got a couple of things ahead of you at the moment." She gestured at the rather large pile of data that was not just filling her in-box but overflowing it, as well.

"I'll call you if I come up with anything," she promised Noelle, putting her hand over the other woman's. The next minute, she shifted her attention to Duncan. "Hey, are you going to be there next weekend for the big event?"

Duncan laughed. He was surprised that she even had to ask. "I couldn't very well not come to my own brother's wedding now, could I? He's the first one from my family to bite the dust."

"What a sensitive way to put it," Brenda commented, then went on to say, "Sometimes it's hard to tell all you Cavanaughs apart without a score card." She turned to look at Noelle. "How about you?" she asked.

Had she missed something? "I'm sorry. How about me what?"

"Are you coming to the wedding?" Brenda asked.

Rather than answer her right away, Noelle glanced at her partner for a further explanation.

"My older brother is getting married next Saturday," Duncan told her, adding what he had already touched on earlier today. "Andrew's having one of those blowout bashes that I told you about."

"They met on the job," Brenda interjected, giving her a little background to flesh the story out. "She thought he was trafficking in underage sex slaves and he thought she was a madam."

"Sounds like love at first sight to me," Noelle quipped. She couldn't help wondering if she'd suddenly gotten sucked into a vortex with facts and occurrences being thrown at her, right and left.

"You know, that's not a bad idea," Duncan said to Brenda, referring to his partner's attendance at his brother's nuptials. "I already told her that I thought Lucy might enjoy the diversion."

"Lucy?" Brenda asked, looking from him to Noelle for an explanation.

"That's my grandmother," she explained. "She won't come right out and admit it, but losing her friends has hit her pretty hard."

"Who can blame her?" Brenda commiserated. "Sounds like a Cavanaugh wedding might be just what the doctor ordered. Oh, and go ahead and bring your daughter," she added. "All the kids will be there at the wedding. Your daughter'll have fun."

Noelle thought that was rather a broad assumption. "You don't know how old she is," she pointed out.

"Doesn't matter," Brenda said. "We've got a wide range of kids coming to the celebration—Andrew wouldn't have it any other way. The kids come in all ages, all sizes. There's bound to be some your daughter can play with. It'll be fun," Brenda promised her, adding with a broad smile, "I've never been to a Cavanaugh party that wasn't."

"She ought to know," Duncan said, adding in his two cents. "Brenda's been attending these functions, gatherings and parties a lot longer than I have."

Wanting to wrap this up and move on with the unofficial case, Duncan told his partner, "Tell you what. I'll pick the three of you up next Saturday at eleven and bring you to the reception if you'd rather skip the ceremony."

He was going to an awful lot of trouble in her opinion. In his place, she would have just scribbled down an address and left him to figure out how to get there himself.

"Won't your date mind you picking us up like that?" she asked.

"As it happens," he explained, "I'm currently between dates. Besides, I wouldn't bring a date to a wedding," he added with feeling. "It might give her ideas."

Brenda laughed and shook her head. "He *thinks* he's a confirmed bachelor," she confided to Noelle in a stage whisper, clearly not of the same opinion about the matter as Duncan was. "I've seen it before," she said. "In case you're wondering, every one of those so-called 'confirmed bachelors' is married now."

This was where he needed to make an exit, Duncan decided. "Some people just have trouble sticking to their convictions," he told Brenda. With that, he turned on his heel. "I'd appreciate getting a call when you have some answers," he said as he walked out.

Noelle had the presence of mind to look over her shoulder at Brenda and say, "Thank you," before she fell into place and followed her partner back to the elevator.

Chapter 6

"A wedding?" Lucy asked in surprise when Noelle broached the subject of Duncan's invitation to her grandmother that evening.

"Yes." They were in the kitchen and Lucy was getting dinner started. Tonight's fare was chicken parmesan, Melinda's favorite. "My partner's brother is getting married next Saturday and we're invited."

"Your partner." Lucy slid the last piece of breaded chicken into the heated frying pan and placed a vented cover to keep the crackling splatter contained. "Is that the tall, good-looking guy who came to Henry's funeral?" her grandmother asked, slanting a knowing glance at her.

Noelle smiled, amused at what seemed to stand

out in her grandmother's mind. "That's him," she confirmed—as if Lucy didn't already know.

Lucy nodded, taking a fork out of the utensil drawer. "You should go."

"The invitation was extended to all three of us. Melinda, too," she added when Lucy looked at her quizzically.

Lucy frowned slightly to herself. "I can see your partner inviting you as his date, but this isn't his reception," she pointed out. "He can't just invite two more people the groom doesn't know."

She had to set her grandmother straight before this got out of hand. Lucy had a tendency to let her imagination run away with her, given half a chance.

"I'm not his date," Noelle began.

"Well, you're not his water boy—or water girl," Lucy amended, then challenged, "If you're not his date, what would you call it?"

"Easy. I'm his plus one," Noelle said for lack of a better term. That was all she needed, to have her grandmother tell people she was "dating" her partner. "And from what I gather, the Cavanaughs do things in a big way. They throw their doors open and yell, 'you-all come on over now,' or something like that and everyone within a twenty-mile radius just turns up, eats and has a general good time."

Okay, so it was an exaggeration, she thought—but not by much. She had never paid attention to the actual dynamics before, so she had pretty much been in the dark about how the Cavanaughs operated, but now that one of them was her partner, she was perforce more in tune to what was going on. The family, from what she could ascertain, went on for miles.

Lucy laughed shortly under her breath. "Certainly wouldn't want to clean up after *that* party," she murmured, lifting the lid from the pan and turning over each piece of chicken so that the other side could be browned. "But I do think that you and Melinda should go. It'll be good for you," she said, looking at Noelle significantly. "You don't get out that much, you know."

Noelle met her grandmother's look head-on. "Right back at you, Lucy."

Lucy waved away the mere suggestion. "I'm not up to it."

Noelle was not about to be put off. She had no real desire to attend a reception where she hardly knew anyone, but her grandmother could use the diversion. "Which is exactly why you should go. And if you're worried about not fitting in, I'm told that Cavanaughs come in all sizes, shapes and ages."

"I've never had a problem fitting in," Lucy informed her.

Well, that settled that, Noelle thought, relieved. "Great, then you'll come."

Lucy began to demur again, then stopped as she apparently thought better of it. "Maybe it might be fun at that," she agreed. The moment she made her decision, Lucy's face lit up.

Noting the look, Noelle felt really pleased. She

hadn't seen Lucy smile like that since Henry's death. It was worth having to deal with feeling awkward at the reception just to see Lucy acting like her old self.

Thanks, Cavanaugh, Noelle thought as she began to set the table. *I owe you one.*

It was hard to say who was more excited about attending this wedding, Noelle thought while she waited for her partner to arrive the following Saturday, Lucy or Melinda. Both her grandmother and her daughter seemed to be unusually energized. Amazingly enough, Melinda had even held still for her while she brushed her daughter's hair to get her ready.

At least Melinda's little body was still. Her mouth, however, was going a mile a minute, asking questions about the wedding, about her partner and about everything in between.

Noelle could hardly keep up, or answer the six-year-old fast enough. Each time she did, another question would pop up.

"How many kids are going to be there?" Melinda asked as she was finishing up with her daughter's hair.

"Hold still, honey," she cautioned. This was the last snag she needed to brush out of the curly red hair. "A lot."

"How many in 'a lot'?" Melinda asked, attempting to turn her head around in order to look up at her.

Placing her hand on Melinda's chin, Noelle deliberately moved her daughter's head so that she faced forward again. "How old did you say you were?" she asked the petite little redhead with a laugh.

Melinda did her best to appear taller than she was. "I'm six. You know that, Momma," the little girl reminded her.

"Yes, I do. What I don't know is the exact number of kids that'll be there. I just know that the Cavanaughs have a lot of kids in their family, so you'll have plenty of company at the reception."

All this time, Lucy had maintained a steadfast post by the bay window, acting as a lookout. "I think our ride's here," she announced just then, glancing over her shoulder at Noelle.

Duncan.

Noelle had absolutely no idea why Lucy's innocent announcement would have her stomach suddenly tightening up as if it were a sweater tossed into a dryer set on Hot. It wasn't as if she hadn't seen him five days a week for more than the past six months.

And besides, this *wasn't* a date, she reminded herself. If it had been, she would have given him some excuse, begged off and as time for the reception drew close, she would have been busy cleaning the kitchen floor or something equally as glamorous and exciting.

She wasn't much on social get-togethers, not since the death of her second fiancé. These days, Lucy and Melinda were more than enough company for her. Dating was part of her past, not the present or the future.

The doorbell rang.

Noelle pressed her lips together. It looked like she was attending this social gathering whether she liked it or not.

"Okay, people," Noelle said, trying to sound as nonchalant as if they were just heading for an outing at the grocery store, "it's showtime."

"We're putting on a show?" Melinda's eyes widening gleefully. "What kind of show?" she asked.

"The kind that'll keep your mom's partner coming back," Lucy told her great-granddaughter, lowering her voice.

She hadn't lowered it enough. "Lucy!" There was a warning note in Noelle's voice.

A note that Lucy made a point of completely ignoring. "No time to talk now, honey. Can't keep the man waiting," she declared, ushering Melinda before her as she opened the front door. "Men don't like to be kept waiting."

"Hi, handsome, we're ready," Lucy greeted Duncan. She nodded at her great-granddaughter, who she had standing directly in front of her. "This little live wire is Melinda. She looks just like Noelle did when Noelle was her age."

"He doesn't need to know that, Lucy," Noelle chided her grandmother.

Lucy was undaunted as she smiled at Duncan.

"Just a little sidebar. I have a *lot* of trivia at my disposal," she confided to Noelle's partner.

"Then I'll know who to come to if I have a question," Duncan quipped. Crouching down to the little girl's level, he went through the motions of a formal introduction. "Hi, Melinda. My name's Duncan."

Like a true little femme fatale in training, Melinda smiled up at him. "Hi. I'm ready to go."

Duncan rose to his feet, fighting the urge to tousle her hair. He had a feeling that a lot had gone into giving the little girl that smooth hairstyle.

"So am I," he replied. And then Duncan glanced in Noelle's direction, actually looking at his partner for the first time since he'd walked in. To his credit, he managed to keep the surprise from registering on his face. But not from his mind.

Damn, she looked good.

When they rode together, for the most part Noelle showed up in jackets, tailored pants and silk, button-down blouses, all very utilitarian. Her hair was usually worn up and was pinned out of the way.

Noelle was wearing her hair down now and it fell to her shoulders in an enticing wave that was reddish with golden highlights. Instead of a suit she was wearing a dark green, above-the-knee dress that managed to find every one of her soft curves and clung to them like a long-lost friend.

"You seen my partner around?" he asked her once he regained the use of his tongue. "I was supposed to meet her here."

"Very funny. You want to change your mind about that invitation?" she asked, thinking maybe this was his way of wiggling out of having to take her to the reception.

"Not a chance," he said with feeling. "You clean up nice, O'Banyon," he told her. His eyes, as they took in every inch of her with slow, languid care, said a great deal more.

Noelle struggled not to blush.

"Momma wasn't dirty," Melinda informed him, confused.

He grinned at the little girl. "My mistake," he said. "All right, ladies, if we're going to make the wedding, we should get going."

Though Melinda looked eager to latch on to him, Duncan paused to offer his arm to the little girl's great-grandmother instead.

Lucy slipped her arm through his and then patted his forearm. "Whoever taught you your manners, Duncan, should be commended."

"Thank you. My mother would have been happy to hear that," he said.

Instant sympathy filled Lucy's eyes as she seemed to understand the unspoken part of Duncan's statement.

The man was a smooth operator, she'd give him that, Noelle thought, locking her door and taking her daughter's hand.

And he'd also been right, she decided, catching a glimpse of her grandmother's profile. This outing was *definitely* good for Lucy, and for that, she was extremely grateful to him.

"Overwhelmed yet?"

The amused question came from a pretty young woman who approached her from the side approximately an hour after Duncan had brought her and her family to the wedding. They had arrived in time to watch Duncan's brother solemnly recite the vows that bound him to Tiana, the woman he'd met while working undercover.

Once the ceremony was over, it was a signal for the intense partying to begin.

But for all the raw, unfiltered energy that abounded all around her as far as she could see, the insanity element which was responsible for abject chaos that overtook better judgment at so many of these kinds of parties was notably missing.

The participants were vibrant, but—possibly because of who they were and what they represented—they were also law-abiding. To a person, Noelle could not help noticing, the people attending this reception were all exemplary partiers.

Noelle, standing momentarily alone, turned around now in response to the question and saw a young woman smiling at her.

The moment their eyes met, the young woman was quick to speak. "Hi, I'm Kelly. If it helps you remember, I'm also Brennan and Duncan's sister," she added, then laughed at Noelle's reaction. "Don't look so worried. There won't be a quiz at the end of the reception," she promised. "This can be a pretty overwhelming group the first few times you encounter them, especially in such numbers. But we're harmless if you remember to feed us. Just kidding," Kelly quickly assured her.

"If you're going to survive this crowd," Kelly counseled, "you're going to have to relax. But then," she amended, "if you've survived so far being Duncan's partner, I guess that I don't really need to give you any advice, do I?"

"Actually," Noelle confided, lowering her voice just a tad, "I'd appreciate any help I can get." She paused, thinking of Duncan and his behavior these past few hours. "Is he always this, um…"

"Pushy?" Kelly guessed, supplying the missing word.

The word wasn't couched in niceties, but it did sum up what she was trying to express. "Well, yes," Noelle finally said.

"No. Actually, he's toned down some," Kelly confided. "He used to be worse. Had to have his way in everything," she confided. "I think becoming a police detective helped him grow up. It was either that or the rest of us were going to kill him."

"Then there's hope for you yet," Duncan told his sister, coming up behind her and his partner. He had two glasses of punch in his hand. He offered one to Noelle and kept the other. "Thought you might need this right about now," he said. "By the way," he confided, inclining his head just a little, "I think your grandmother is charming my grand-uncle, or vice versa," he allowed, nodding in the couple's general direction.

Noelle looked over to where he'd indicated. Sure enough, Lucy was talking to an older man with the thickest mane of silver hair she'd seen in a while. It made her think of a lion, holding court. Lucy appeared to be truly enjoying herself. Coming here had been a good thing, Noelle thought, pleased.

"Hey, where's my glass of punch?" Kelly asked.

"Probably still in the bowl would be my guess," Duncan anwered, not rising to his sister's bait. "Better go get it before it's all gone."

"It's never 'all gone' at Andrew's house," Thomas Cavanaugh, one of Duncan's newly discovered relatives said, walking by the two of them. "The man seems to always have this endless supply of whatever it is you're looking for." Nodding at Noelle, he introduced himself. "Hi, I'm Thomas."

"I'm Noelle." She flashed a smile at him, but it was easy to see that she was getting very confused by all the faces at the reception. "Is there some huge cloning device hidden on the property somewhere?" she asked Duncan after she took a sip of her punch.

"I'll let you field that one," Kelly told Duncan. "Me, I've got a punch bowl to find." Nodding at her, Kelly took her leave.

"We do tend to look somewhat alike," Duncan agreed. "But if you take a really good look at any of us standing side by side, you'll be able to see the differences," he assured her.

Noelle sincerely doubted that.

"If you say so," she murmured without much conviction. Right about now, scores of names and faces were all swimming aimlessly in her mind's eye. "I want to thank you again for inviting Lucy," she said more seriously. She glanced over at her grandmother and Shamus, the family patriarch she was talking to. The two seemed to be very much in a world of their own. Looking at the duo, Noelle smiled to herself. From this distance, her grandmother looked almost like a young girl, flirting with a boyfriend. "She really does seem to be having a good time."

"I figured as much," he said casually. "Rumor has it that no one's ever had a bad time at one of these gatherings." As he spoke to her, Duncan noticed the way Noelle appeared to be scanning the area, her eyes darting from one cluster of kids to another on the wide back lawn. "She's over there." He pointed out a rather large group of children playing right next to the gaily decorated gazebo.

Melinda appeared to be smack in the center of the group. Even at this distance, Noelle could see her daughter was having a very good time.

"She commands attention," Duncan commented.

Noelle wasn't about to argue that. "She gets that from her great-grandmother," she told him.

"And what does she get from her mother?" he asked, surprising her. What he said next surprised her even more. "I mean besides those incredible green eyes and that dazzling grin."

Suddenly embarrassed, Noelle demurred, "I don't have either."

Duncan's expression was incredulous. "They take away all the mirrors in your house, O'Banyon?" he asked. "Because from where I'm standing, that was a pretty accurate assessment on my part."

Instead of avoiding his eyes, she did an about-face and met his head-on. "You practicing, Cavanaugh?" she asked him, trying her best to sound distant.

It would have been all too easy to allow herself to believe he meant what he'd just said, believe that this was a date not with her partner, but with the drop-dead gorgeous guy that he was. And that, she knew would have been a very fatal mistake—for him and most especially, for her. They meshed well as part-ners. She couldn't sacrifice that because being with him made her feel an itch she wanted so desperately to scratch.

He didn't follow her meaning. "Practicing?" he repeated, waiting for some sort of clarification.

"For when you go out on a real date," she sup-plied. "I realize I'm just a place holder, but I guess you decided to get in a little practice time on me so the day's not a total loss."

"You were a 'place holder,'" he allowed. "But place holders are made of cardboard—and you're not. Moreover, I have to admit, I'm having a pretty good time," he told her.

What was left mostly unsaid was that he was having that good time with *her*.

But it was understood.

"Yeah," she heard herself admitting, her voice sounding a little reedy and high, "me, too."

Because looking into his eyes was having a very strange effect on her, Noelle shifted her gaze and looked down into the glass she was holding instead. The late afternoon sunshine danced and shimmered across the surface like trapped sunbeams.

"I guess that means there's something in this punch, huh?" she asked, attempting to laugh off what she'd just said.

"Just juice," he assured her.

Noelle took a breath. "I guess I just can't hold my juice," she murmured.

Duncan grinned. "I guess not." Then, to her surprise, he took the glass he'd recently given her out of her hand and placed it on the nearest table. He put his own right next to it.

Though she'd surrendered her glass, Noelle watched him rather uncertainly. "What are you doing?"

"Can't you hear it?" he asked. When she made no response, he nodded his head toward the speakers. "They're playing our song."

Okay, time to pull back a little. There were boundaries that had to be reaffirmed. Otherwise, working with Cavanaugh might be a problem come Monday morning.

"We don't have a song, Cavanaugh," Noelle needlessly reminded him.

"Then I guess we'll have to make it this one," he said.

The next thing she knew, Noelle found herself dancing—and having what she could only assess as an out-of-body experience.

With Duncan.

Chapter 7

"But I don't dance," Noelle insisted.

The tune was fast and catchy and there were a fair amount of couples dancing on the makeshift dance floor some of his siblings had put together solely for this occasion.

Duncan had pulled her out in the middle of the crowd as if to discourage her refusal.

It worked.

If she walked off now, she'd cause a minor scene. That was not something she would have wanted to be remembered for, especially since this was a Cavanaugh wedding and she was, after all, very much the outsider despite how friendly everyone was being.

They all knew each other. She just knew Duncan—
and Brian, the chief of d's, but strictly by sight.

The expression in her partner's eyes as he lowered
them to hers said he wasn't buying into her protest.

"Funny, your feet haven't gotten that message." He
pretended to look down at them now as if to check.
"Sure looks like dancing to me. C'mon, O'Banyon,
loosen up a little. Let yourself go," he urged. "That's
what these kinds of gatherings are for, you know. To
knock off some steam."

"I thought it was to celebrate your brother's wedding," she reminded him.

"That, too. No law against doing both, you know,"
Duncan told her.

"What if I don't want to knock off any steam?"
she challenged.

He shook his head. "Well, seeing that you're
wound up tighter than anyone I've ever met, if you
don't let off any steam, then you're going to just
blow up someday." Because the din was growing, he
leaned into her and said, "You don't want that happening." She looked far from won over, so he added,
"You've got a little girl to raise."

"And you'd be the expert on that. Raising a daughter," she said when he raised a quizzical eyebrow at
her comeback.

Instead of being put off, he took her words in
stride. "Maybe not specifically, but I'm pretty much
of an expert on being part of a family and how things
devolve when the dynamics change for the worse."

Duncan paused for a moment, debating just how much to say as he moved about the dance area with her. He decided she'd probably find out eventually, so he might as well use the story to make a point.

"My mother died when I was a kid. Still had a father, still had siblings and more cousins, aunts and uncles than any three average kids, but I missed her. I felt the lack of her in my life. Actually, I still do," he concluded.

Noelle felt awkward in the face of the unexpected revelation. She wasn't very good when it came to expressing sympathy, even though he had relayed the information to her rather casually.

Because, despite the music, there was a stillness hanging between them she felt she *had* to say something. "I'm sorry you lost your mother," she murmured. "But at least you had one."

He looked at her in surprise. "I thought you did, too."

"Oh, I did," she agreed. "Had a father, too. But mostly in name only." Her mouth curved ruefully. "I got in the way of their travel plans. They kept leaving me with Lucy whenever they went out of town and picking me up when they got back." She shrugged, gazing off at nothing in particular. "One day, they just conveniently forgot to pick me up. I lived with Lucy after that." This time her smile was genuine. "Turned out better that way for everyone. Lucy liked feeling useful and I stopped feeling as if I was always in the way. And my parents felt free again," she added as an afterthought.

He decided she could use a change of subject. "Melinda seems like an adjusted, happy little girl," he observed.

Her face softened as she thought of her daughter. "Thank you. She is. I couldn't have done that without my parents," she confided.

He drew his head back and looked at her, puzzled. That didn't make any sense. "I thought you said—"

She was quick to explain her thinking. "I just remember everything they did and then I do the opposite. If I want an *actual* role model, I just look to Lucy. The song stopped," she announced abruptly.

To her surprise, Duncan didn't loosen his hold on her. "It's like a city bus in a metropolitan area," he said easily. "There'll be another one right along." The small band his uncle had hired began to play again. Duncan smiled. "Ah, see, what did I say?"

The tempo was exceedingly languid. "It's a slow dance," Noelle pointed out.

"Good. Less dancing required on your part." He looked into her face and his smile seemed to engulf her. "Not that you don't dance a lot better than you think you do. You probably do a lot of things better than you give yourself credit for," he guessed.

Noelle felt a strange queasiness starting in her stomach and rippling all through her.

Pep talk notwithstanding, she felt herself all but melting against him. There was something hot and potentially unmanageable growing in direct proportion to her closeness to him.

She silently lectured herself. Reacting to Cavanaugh, in any manner, shape or form except strictly professionally had absolutely no future for her.

She was well aware of that.

Besides, she'd gone this long, more than six years, without so much as even feeling a vague tingle in response to a man.

So what was going on with her now?

Why him?

Because you haven't been in a situation that could be described as even remotely social since Christopher's death. Right now you're half-dressed, pressed up against a hard body and swaying to the music while his arms are around you. You haven't been pronounced dead yet, so what do you expect?

"Is that a private conversation or can anyone join in?" Duncan asked, breaking into her thoughts.

Caught off guard, Noelle blinked, drawing her head back to look at him. "What?"

"That conversation you're obviously having in your head. I can almost *feel* it going on against my shoulder. I was just wondering if you were going to keep it to yourself or share at least some of it with the class," her partner teased.

"No private conversation," she denied. Because he was waiting for some sort of an explanation, she grabbed at the first one she could think of. "I'm just wondering why you're not dancing with someone else."

"Why should I find someone else when I'm perfectly happy with the partner I have?" he asked. It tickled him to see a bit of color creeping up along her collarbone. "So tell me, Detective O'Banyon, what other hidden talents do you have?"

"Hidden talents?" she echoed. She shook her head, not getting his meaning.

"Well, you dance better than just okay," he said, "you're very loyal to your family, make a great mother from what I can see and you clean up *really* well. I was just wondering if there's anything else I should know about you."

Flirting. He was flirting with her. She couldn't believe it. Didn't the man know better? "I did very well in my martial arts classes," she told him by way of a warning.

The warning didn't go far. "You did? How about that? Me, too," he said cheerfully. "We should have an all-out match sometime, see who wins." He made it sound as if he would relish the confrontation. She didn't know if he was putting her on—or if he was serious.

The one thing she did know was that she couldn't appear to back off. So her eyes met his and she told him, "Sounds good to me."

But when Duncan smiled into her eyes and said in a lowered, sensual voice, "Me, too," Noelle did back off, thinking that if she went any further with this proposal to match their martial arts skills, she might be biting off more than she could chew.

Failure was not an option she relished. And with him, she knew she'd never live it down.

This time, when the music stopped, she deliberately slipped her hands from his. "I'd better go check on Lucy and Melinda."

Duncan quickly caught her hand as the band began to play yet another song. "Your daughter's obviously having fun and I have a hunch that Lucy wouldn't take kindly to her granddaughter checking up on her, especially since she and my grandfather's brother haven't stopped talking to each other and laughing like a couple of college kids in the last hour."

Noelle looked first where her daughter was playing with about eleven other children and then over toward Lucy, who was sitting on a swing with the man Duncan had introduced to her as his late grandfather's brother, Shamus. Everyone seemed rather contented to be exactly where they were.

Like you, a voice in her head said.

No, not like her, Noelle silently insisted. She did what she could to resist both the voice and the thought it was promoting. Because she wasn't contented. She couldn't allow herself to be. Contentment made you drop your guard and allowed you to be at your most vulnerable.

She'd been vulnerable more times than she cared to recall and the sensation was highly overrated—not to mention rather dangerous to both her state of mind and her body, since things happened to her when she was vulnerable. Sad, soul-numbing things she didn't want to be put in a position to experience again.

She needed to keep her guard up, Noelle told herself firmly. Otherwise, who knew what was going to go wrong next?

She didn't want to find out.

Abruptly, before the band stopped playing, she pulled her hands from his.

He saw the strange look in her eyes. Was that fear? Her? He had to be imagining things. He had already learned that his partner could be pretty gutsy.

"Something wrong?" he asked.

"Nothing's wrong," she answered.

"We're the only ones on the dance floor standing still," he pointed out. "That qualifies as something being wrong in my book."

"I just suddenly need some punch," Noelle explained, grasping at the first excuse she could think of.

Rather than talk her out of it or laugh at her flimsy excuse, Duncan surprised her by going along with it.

"Okay, then let's 'suddenly' go get some punch," he said gamely. Taking her hand, he led her from the dance floor toward the table where he'd left their glasses. The half-empty glasses were still there.

"Ah, nice to know you can still count on some things," Duncan said, turning around with a glass in each hand. "Just where we left them."

"Which one's mine?" she asked, looking from one glass to the other. They both contained approximately the same amount of punch.

Duncan looked at the glasses he held in his hands. "Why should that matter?" he asked her. "Mine wasn't spiked and the last time around, the department doctor gave me a clean bill of health so I don't have anything you can catch—unless you have something *I* can catch. Do you have any communicable diseases?" he said brightly.

She found the very suggestion appalling and made no effort to hide that. "No!"

"Then fine." He held out the two glasses to her. "Pick your poison—so to speak."

She shook her head, rejecting both glasses. "I think I'll just go get a fresh glass of punch if you don't mind."

"I don't mind at all," he answered her amicably. "But I am a little curious about what you're afraid of, O'Banyon."

What she was "afraid of," Noelle realized, was that if she drank out of his glass, it would amount to being one step closer to intimacy. It would be too much like her lips touching his and that would be breaching a barrier she didn't want to cross.

Noelle sighed, pressing her lips together.

She might not want to have her barriers breached, but at the same time, she'd always been the kid who took dares, the woman who met each and every challenge head-on. The fastest way to get her to do something was to say that she couldn't do it or that she would fail ignobly in the attempt.

With Duncan's question about fear still ringing in her ears, she turned on her heel and marched back to her partner. Taking the glass out of his right hand, Noelle drained what was left in it.

Then, for good measure, she took the glass he had in his other hand. Tilting it back, she drained that glass, as well.

She thrust both glasses back into his hands. "Satisfied?"

"Well, not really," he admitted, keeping a straight face. "Now I don't have anything to drink. Guess we'll have to get two fresh glasses after all," he said cheerfully, walking by her as he made his way to the closest refreshment table.

Staring after his departing back, Noelle shook her head. She was letting him get to her and she didn't even know why—or how to keep it from happening on an ongoing basis.

"Here, let me have her," Lucy urged, holding her arms out for her great-granddaughter.

It was a little past ten o'clock and Duncan had driven them back to Noelle's house. Though she'd tried very hard to keep her eyes opened, Melinda had finally lost the battle and fallen asleep—hard. So hard that she hadn't woken up as Duncan carefully got her out of her car seat and then carried her into the house.

"I can carry Melinda upstairs," Noelle's grandmother told him. With a warm smile she added, "You've done more than enough for the O'Banyon women today. I just want you to know that I had a lovely time."

After she gently removed the sleeping child from his arms, Lucy kissed the top of Melinda's head and began to head for the stairs.

Taking care of her daughter was *her* job, Noelle thought, snapping to attention. Certainly not a task to be delegated.

"She's too heavy for you, Lucy," Noelle protested. "I'll take her."

"She's not too heavy yet. So unless you want to turn this child into a tug-of-war toy, I suggest you let me have my way." her grandmother argued. "Thanks again," she said, tossing the words over her shoulder toward Duncan just before she began to climb up the stairs.

Duncan stood at the foot of the staircase for a minute, watching the woman ascend with her sleeping great-granddaughter in her arms. Lucy moved like the very embodiment of strength, he couldn't help thinking. The woman was nothing if not admirably capable.

"Your grandmother's really something else," he told Noelle as he moved away from the stairs.

He wasn't about to get an argument from her. "Don't I know it," Noelle agreed with a laugh. "But what she just said goes double for me," she went on to tell him. He cocked his head, silently asking her to elaborate. So she did. "Thanks for today. Lucy and Melinda both had an absolute ball."

"How about you?" he asked as he made his way back to the front door with Noelle shadowing his steps. "What did you have?"

Several quips came to mind as a response, but she refrained from saying any of them. He deserved the truth if nothing else.

"Fun," she finally answered, and as the word left her lips, she realized how true that actually was. She'd had fun, just pure fun. As had Melinda and Lucy. And she knew she had him to thank for that. "You have a really nice family."

Duncan nodded. "Yeah, which is pretty fortunate because I don't think I can give them back at this point. I've gotten too much mileage out of them." Reaching the door, he turned around to face her and paused for a moment. "It was nice hearing you laugh," he said. "You should do it more often."

Noelle shrugged self-consciously. She didn't know how to handle compliments. She didn't get them much in her line of work.

"Our job's not funny," she pointed out.

"Humor is really important. It's what sees us through the worst of any situation. You lose your sense of humor, the bad guys win. Think about it," he urged when he saw the skeptical look blossom on her face.

"Yeah, well, I will think about it," she promised, then felt compelled to ask, "Um, do you want a nightcap or anything?" She felt that she needed to offer him something in exchange for the invitation to Brennan's wedding he'd bestowed on her and hers.

For a moment, Duncan was sorely tempted, not by the offer, but for the excuse to linger a little longer with this softer, more amicable version of his partner. But then he glanced at his wristwatch. The hour hand was flirting with eleven. He needed to call it a night—and so did she.

"Thanks, but it's getting late and I've got a full day ahead of me tomorrow. You probably do, too."

She nodded at his excuse as she put her hand on the doorknob and turned it. "Thanks again for inviting us."

"Thanks again for coming," Duncan countered.

Then, to Noelle's surprise, he leaned in and brushed a kiss against her cheek. "See you Monday," he told her just before he walked away.

Noelle stood there in the open doorway, watching her partner as he made his way down the front walk to his vehicle, got into it and then drove off.

She stood there as Duncan's six-year-old white sedan became progressively smaller and smaller, then disappeared as he made a right-hand turn two streets down to leave the development.

And she remained there longer than that. She stood there, riveted, until the area where his lips had touched her skin finally ceased throbbing and the warmth finally, *finally* started to fade away.

Only then did she close the door and go up to her room.

Chapter 8

For the most part, Noelle had always prided herself on the fact that she was always on time, if not early, to everything. This included foremost her job, any appointment she might have, as well as the occasional lunch date she made to meet friends.

As a rule, she didn't like to be kept waiting and hated to be the person who kept anyone else waiting. Punctuality was a mainstay in her life.

Unless something unforeseen came up to delay her.

Like this morning.

She'd started out this morning the way she did every morning, by leaving early. This despite the fact that she'd had less than an acceptable amount of sleep. Her grandmother, still riding high on the day she had spent with the Cavanaugh family, most notably their patriarch, Shamus, had spent both Saturday night and Sunday night at her house rather than driving home to her small apartment. Still hyped up on enthusiasm, Lucy had talked a blue streak, reiterating her conversation with Shamus practically verbatim with added sidebars, comments and opinions on everything and anything that had transpired from the moment they had set foot on the Cavanaugh grounds.

It had been a long time since she had seen her grandmother that happy, so Noelle couldn't bring herself to beg off and go to bed even on Sunday night. Not until Lucy finally ran out of steam.

By then it was a little after midnight.

But even so, sleep turned out to be a reluctant guest in her bedroom and when it finally did make an appearance, it brought a cache of unsettling dreams along with it. Dreams that Noelle staunchly refused to analyze or even review once she was awake.

Dreams about things she had absolutely no business even *thinking,* she'd silently upbraided herself.

But even this rather acute absence of sleep wasn't what was responsible for making her arrive late to the precinct this Monday morning.

The blame belonged exclusively to the accident. The one that had a weathered Escalade melding with a utility pole on the side of the road. It wasn't even that the wreck impeded her travels. The car, or what was left of it, was out of the way of general traffic.

It was what she *saw* that ultimately caused her to be late. And the unnerving fact that this accident was occurring not that far away from the seniors' home where Henry had died—or been "helped" to die.

Driving carefully by, she kept as far to the left as she could to avoid getting in the way of the first responders on the scene of the accident. Force of habit had Noelle looking in the direction of the wrecked car. As she looked, she was fervently hoping that there were no casualties.

But there were. The arrival of the coroner's vehicle testified to that. One casualty, the lone occupant of the van. The driver.

Just as she was about to drive past the scene, Noelle saw the gurney with its depressing black body bag being lowered off the back of the coroner's van.

That was when she saw the victim who had been lifted out from behind the wheel of his crumpled Escalade and placed on the ground.

It was a man who had seen at least seven decades pass by.

She wasn't sure exactly what possessed her to pull over. There was nothing she could do to help; she was aware of that from the start. Heaven knew there were enough fire and police personnel about to more than handle the situation twice over.

But the age of the victim had red flags going up in her head. There were questions she needed to have answered.

Parking her vehicle on the same side as the victim's smashed SUV and the coroner's black van, Noelle got out and crossed over to where the body was lying on the ground, still uncovered.

"Lady, you can't stop here," a uniformed policeman informed her authoritatively, shifting over so that he placed himself directly between her and the dead driver.

Noelle held up her shield and ID for the policeman to check out.

"It's okay. I'm on the job." She never took her eyes off the exceptionally bloodied man on the ground. "What happened?" she asked.

In the presence of a detective, the policeman became infinitely friendlier and relaxed. His entire countenance changed.

"As near as I can figure it, I think the guy had a heart attack. I don't know if that was before or after he lost control of the car. Probably before," he guessed, and then the man's expression became rather wry. "But it all depends on which 'eyewitness' you talk to." He jerked a thumb at the two people, a man and a woman, whose statements were presently being taken by another policeman. "They're married and they can't seem to agree on anything."

Turning back to look at Noelle, the policeman asked, "You know him, Detective?" indicating the dead man.

Noelle shook her head. "No, I don't."

He looked at her. "Then why…?"

She anticipated the rest of his question. She

couldn't say anything about a gut feeling, or Lucy's two dead friends. That was a conversation that was a couple of levels above the man's pay grade, so she said the only thing she could, given the situation. "I just stopped to see if you needed any help."

He seemed duly impressed by the offer, even as he turned it down. "Thanks, but we've got it under control, Detective."

She nodded, scarcely hearing him. She was watching the coroner's team place the body into the black body bag and zip it up. She could almost hear the words *the end* being whispered by the black vinyl.

Maybe she was just losing her mind.

Turning toward the coroner, Noelle took out one of her cards and held it out to the man. "Could you let me know what your findings turn out to be when you do your autopsy?"

The coroner perused the business card and then regarded her. The frown he wore like a badge deepened. "You think there's something wrong, Detective?"

"Other than the man being dead? I don't know," she answered truthfully. "But the autopsy should help me find that out."

With that, Noelle withdrew and walked back to her car.

There was no reason for her to think that what she'd just come across was anything but an unfortunate accident. One that could have been so much worse under different circumstances. It was all probably just a simple matter: The man was driving and had a heart attack, most likely the result of years of poor eating habits, insufficient exercise and far too few medical exams that could have put him ahead of the problem.

But even going over those plausible explanations didn't placate her. The whole incident made her uneasy.

It was still bothering her half an hour later when she finally arrived at work.

Glancing at her watch as she got out of her car in the parking lot, she realized that she was five minutes late. Not exactly earth-shattering, but still not something she wanted anyone to take note of.

Noelle hurried up the back steps, fairly flew into the building and then, rather than waiting for the elevator, she decided to take the stairs to the third floor. It was faster.

Just a tad out of breath because of her pace, Noelle strode down the hall and into the squad room.

Cavanaugh, she noticed, was already at his desk.

The minute she crossed the threshold, he looked in her direction. It was as if he was waiting for her to materialize.

Why?

Was he going to say something about Saturday? Make a comment about her apparent reaction to what could only be cataloged as the most innocent of kisses?

To her surprise, it turned out to have nothing to do with any of that.

The moment she slid into her chair and murmured "Good morning," Duncan responded by asking her, "Why'd you ask the coroner to send you a copy of that traffic victim's autopsy?"

Dumbfounded, Noelle was rendered almost speechless. It took her a couple of seconds to pull her wits together in order to make some sort of a response that didn't involve babbling or the repetition of disjointed words.

She stared at her partner. How could he possibly know that? "What, do you have me wired?"

Duncan shook his head. "Don't have to. You should know by now that there are practically no secrets in the police department."

She sighed, still rather mystified. She knew that some news traveled fast, but this had to be some kind of a record.

"Apparently."

"The coroner called Jamieson to find out what his interest was in the dead man just off the 5 Freeway. Jamieson played it by ear and backed you up—he's got all our backs," Duncan readily told her. "But I've got a hunch that he's going to have a few questions for you—"

"O'Banyon," Jamieson called out. When she turned to look toward the lieutenant, she saw that he was standing in his doorway, beckoning to her. "A word."

"—right about now," Duncan concluded, getting up.

From what she could tell, Cavanaugh was about to follow her. But the lieutenant had only asked her to come to his office.

"Where are you going?" she asked Duncan as she started to head toward the lieutenant's office.

"With you," he answered. When she looked at him, confused, he said, "Hey, in case this hasn't sunken in yet after all this time, we're a team. That means that anything that concerns you, concerns me—and vice versa. Understand?"

Oh, she understood all right, but did he? This could mean trouble. "Even if it arouses Jamieson's displeasure?"

"Even then," he confirmed with no hesitation. "You really don't understand how this works, do you?" he asked her.

"I'm learning," she said solemnly. It went without saying that she was also grateful for the moral support.

Jamieson had withdrawn into his office and was sitting behind his desk, waiting. Noelle stopped just short of the threshold to brace herself, then walked into the lieutenant's office.

Jamieson glanced at Noelle's six-foot-one shadow.

"You decided to bring your bodyguard along?" the lieutenant deadpanned.

"Strictly my idea, Lieu," Duncan said as he took a seat. He watched as his partner slowly lowered herself into the remaining one. "This way, you won't have to repeat yourself later, or need to say anything twice. Saves time," Duncan told his superior cheerfully.

"You were always the thoughtful one," Jamieson said, a touch of sarcasm in his voice. His attention shifted back to the detective he'd actually *called* into his office. "What's the matter, O'Banyon? You don't find your work challenging enough? Or maybe you don't like it here?"

"I like being here just fine, sir," Noelle replied in a clip voice more suited to an enlisted man addressing their sergeant than a police detective speaking to her superior.

"Then why are you asking the coroner to forward his autopsy findings on some poor guy who bought the farm while driving his overpriced car?" the lieutenant asked.

Noelle wet her lips as she slanted a glance at Duncan.

The woman, Duncan thought, had absolutely no idea how appealing she looked just now.

"A hunch, sir," Noelle answered the lieutenant's question. "I had a hunch."

"About?" There was no indication on Jamieson's face what he thought of her response.

Noelle took another breath, hoping her answer wasn't going to anger Jamieson. "I know this is going to sound crazy, but—this is the third old person who's died recently."

Jamieson's brow furrowed as he tried to make sense of what she was saying. "You knew him?"

"No, sir," she admitted.

The furrows became deeper. "Then why—"

"It's complicated, sir," she said, trying to head off his question.

"Apparently. Try to uncomplicate it for me," the lieutenant urged.

Noelle explained her action the only way she knew how, by starting at the beginning. "My grandmother had two old friends who died recently. Both were in good physical condition."

"Until they died," Jamieson concluded with a touch of irony.

Duncan decided that his partner might need a lifeline right about now. "I think what O'Banyon's forgetting to mention is that both people recently took out life insurance policies."

The lieutenant's attention shifted to his senior detective. "And you think they were killed for the payout?"

It was Noelle who answered the question, just as Duncan had hoped she would. "I don't know, sir. I do know that they didn't have any next of kin to leave the money to."

It was obvious that the lieutenant was trying to tie the pieces together to make sense of what was being said.

"And when you saw this accident this morning—"

"It just seemed like too much of a coincidence,"

she told him. "And I don't believe in coincidences. I felt that I should look into the matter, get as much information as I could."

"Don't you have department paperwork to catch up on?" Jamieson reminded her pointedly.

She knew he was telling her to get her priorities straight and she wanted to assure him that she already had. "I'm doing it, sir. This is just something I'm looking into on the side."

The expression on Jamieson's face conveyed deep doubts.

"There's more at play here than just simple homicide, Lieu." Duncan threw his weight behind his partner's budding theory.

Jamieson shifted his chair so that he was facing Duncan. "Go ahead."

Duncan began to make it up as he went along. "We could look at it from the point of view that this is someone's idea of a deadly scam. Talking senior citizens into signing up for insurance policies, maybe offering them some kind of incentive to do it, then getting them to sign over the final death benefits on their policies to some organization or foundation that was advantageous to these people."

He could see that he had gotten the lieutenant's wheels spinning. Duncan built on that. "If nothing else, we could look into it as being some kind of insurance fraud or a scam."

"Or something more fatal than that," Noelle interjected. If she closed her eyes, she could still see the way Lucy had looked, standing over Henry's casket. She wanted to *really* probe into the matter. She owed it not just to those dead people, but to Lucy, as well.

"Well, if the investigation turns up evidence that points to these people deliberately being targeted and marked for termination, then we'll turn what we found over to Homicide," Jamieson informed her.

She understood that, understood boundaries. She wasn't in this for points or some sense of competition. She just wanted the matter exposed and stopped if murder was the endgame.

"And until then?" Noelle prodded.

"Until then, as long as you get that pile of paperwork on your desk done on time, you're free to investigate your little heart out," Jamieson told her. What he said next had her mouth all but dropping open. "You can take the lead on this."

About to rise to her feet to take her leave, she froze over what Jamieson had said. Gripping the chair's armrests, her fingers drew slack and she sank back down into the seat. Her knees had turned into rubber bands.

Noelle stared at the lieutenant, hardly able to blink. "Lead?" she echoed, stunned.

"Unless you don't feel qualified," he replied, watching her reaction.

Lead.

She had never taken lead on a case before. That had always been Duncan's position when it was just the two of them investigating a case. The few times they'd been part of a larger group effort involving a case, lead had belonged to whoever had requested additional help with the investigation.

The thought of being the one in charge of an investigation thrilled and humbled Noelle at the same time.

"No, sir," she told Jamieson quickly. "I mean, yes, sir." This was definitely not coming out right, she thought. "I mean, I feel very qualified to take the lead on this."

"Well, see that you are," Jamieson instructed gruffly, then tacked on a warning. "And that your ego doesn't wind up getting in the way."

Wow. Lead. "No, sir. No ego," she promised, all but crossing her heart.

"You can go now," Jamieson said, waving her out of the office.

As both detectives began to leave the room, Jamieson had one final thing to say—but not to both of them. "Cavanaugh." Duncan paused just inside the office to look at the lieutenant, waiting for him to say what he had to say. "Keep an eye on her," Jamieson ordered him.

"Always, sir," Duncan responded.

Jamieson knew the strengths and weaknesses of all the people under him. "A *professional* eye," Jamieson underscored.

Duncan merely grinned in response. "Sure thing, Lieu." He saw the lieutenant roll his eyes and had the good sense to pretend that he didn't. Instead, Duncan quickly made his way out of the man's office.

"So how does it feel, being the lead on a case for the first time?" Duncan asked his partner once they had gotten back to their respective desks and sat down.

She still felt as if her feet weren't quite touching the ground yet. The import of what had just happened in Jamieson's office was going to take a while to hit and sink in.

The first word that came to her in response to Cavanaugh's question was an honest one. "Scary. It feels scary," she admitted.

"Good," Duncan replied with an approving nod of his head.

She didn't think that she followed that or got his meaning. Was he gloating at her jitters? She didn't think so. From what she knew about him, he really wasn't that type. So what was he saying to her?

"Why?"

"Because if it's scary," he explained patiently, wanting to guide her, but not push, "then it hasn't gone to your head and it means that you want to do a good job. Wanting something is halfway to getting it," he told Noelle.

That sounded like something out of a fortune cookie. But that didn't mean that it wasn't a sound piece of advice. She only hoped that Cavanaugh was right this time.

"So," he was saying. "What's our first move?"

Good question, she thought. Now all she needed was a good answer.

Chapter 9

She was a good detective, Noelle told herself. Granted she didn't have years of experience to draw on, but she felt that she did have good instincts and a feel for this kind of work.

So why was she even hesitating about diving into this new venture and being lead on a case *she* had brought to the lieutenant's attention?

What was the worst thing that could happen if she assumed the reins? She could make a mistake?

Hell, everyone made mistakes, she upbraided herself. The trick was not to let that paralyze you, to learn from it and move on, right?

Putting her mental debate to rest, she braced herself, looked at her partner and "dove" in.

"Step one would be to find out the victim's name and get some kind of background information on him, like whether or not he'd recently taken out a life insurance policy on himself. Then we'll know that we're on to something."

Noelle paused, her eyes meeting his. Waiting for her partner's response. It wasn't that she was seeking Duncan's approval—exactly. She wanted to find out if he would proceed the same way if the shots were his to call.

"Sounds good to me," he said.

She realized that she'd been holding her breath and released it now.

"Okay, then let's go see if the coroner can do something besides pick up a phone and complain," Noelle said, grabbing her jacket and the container of coffee she'd brought in. She hadn't even had a chance to take the lid off of it yet and she had a feeling she was going to need at least several shots of caffeine to keep herself going.

"That's the first step," he agreed as they left the squad room. "But you also might want to talk to the medical examiner, as well." When Noelle gave him a confused glance, Duncan explained, "It's the M.E. who's going to be able to do an autopsy. The coroner just investigates the circumstances to see if anything suspicious occurred."

Noelle pressed the down button for the elevator. She wasn't about to admit this out loud, but this was her first rodeo involving dead bodies. She was at somewhat of a disadvantage.

The elevator arrived and they got in. "Aren't they interchangeable?" Noelle asked despite the fact that she was aware her question drew attention to her ignorance in this department. But her desire to do this right far outweighed her need to save face. She was in charge of a bona fide case and she meant to do right by it.

Getting out in the subbasement, they made their way to the city's morgue. "I wouldn't say that around the M.E. if I were you. He had to get a medical degree to do what he's doing. The coroner just had to prove that he had a pulse and was capable of making a better judgment call than the deceased he'd transported."

"Oh. Thanks," she said belatedly.

Duncan grinned. "Don't mention it. Always glad to help out."

It took them several twists and turns before they finally arrived at the coroner's office. Duncan knocked once, then opened the door. He stepped back to allow Noelle a chance to enter first.

She glanced at him. "I don't know if you're being chivalrous or using me as a decoy."

He laughed. "A little of both," he answered.

She believed him.

The encounter was immediate.

"You again?" The coroner, Edwin Addams, demanded the moment she walked in. He appeared far from happy to see her, even if it was on his own turf.

Noelle tried not to shiver as she walked into the cold, antiseptic area where Addams and his two assistants stored the bodies of citizens who had died on the streets and freeways of Aurora. What amounted to metal drawers were the temporary resting places for the deceased until the next of kin or a friend came to identify them and had their bodies picked up by a funeral home.

"Me again," Noelle replied. It was probably a toss-up as to who didn't want to see whom more. "We need an ID on the victim you picked up this morning."

Addams gave no indication that he was about to move or give her what she wanted. "What division did you say you were with again?"

Just who did he think he was kidding? He'd called her lieutenant. "You know perfectly well what division I'm with," she told him, "or did you just call every division head after you got in this morning, hoping to reach the right person eventually?"

"Okay, you got me," the coroner admitted, not bothering to hide his irritation. "So how is a senior citizen's heart attack Vice's concern? You think he was transporting drugs and decided to take a hit before delivery?" Addams asked her sarcastically.

"We're investigating possible repercussions coming out of an insurance fraud scheme," Duncan answered before she could. He was standing directly behind her and his bodyguard stance was difficult to miss.

The coroner looked from Duncan to Noelle and then back again. He shook his head. "Fraud, huh? Still don't see it."

"That's because it's not your job, it's ours," Duncan said flatly. "Your job is to send the victim's body over to the M.E. so that we can get a better handle on exactly what happened during the guy's last couple of minutes."

Addams scowled. "Just a big waste of time if you ask me."

"But we didn't ask you," Noelle pointed out. They'd already spent too much time here and she wanted to get moving. "Where are the deceased's personal effects?" she asked, looking around for the body. There were several gurneys in the room, but they all appeared to be unoccupied at the moment.

So where was the accident victim?

"His personal effects are with the deceased," one of the coroner's assistants, Silas, volunteered.

Duncan turned to the tall, painfully thin man who the coroner was glaring at. "And where is he?" he asked.

The assistant pointed toward the far wall. From where they were standing, it appeared to be a wide, built-in file cabinet.

Duncan and Noelle immediately crossed to the metal doors. Noelle looked back at Addams and his assistant. "Which one is he in?"

The coroner made no attempt to join them where they were standing. Instead, he held his ground and crossed his thick arms across his even thicker chest.

"Why don't you try your luck and see if you can find him?" he suggested haughtily. It was clear that Addams didn't appreciate being challenged or having his domain breached and he was definitely not about to help them finding *anything*.

Glaring down into the lifeless face of a dead man was not something she relished doing. Searching for the accident victim by playing musical doors made the prospect that much more unappetizing.

As it turned out, she didn't have to look for the accident victim.

Behind her, she heard Duncan telling the coroner, "By the way, I don't think I identified myself to you when we came in. I'm Detective Duncan Cavanaugh." He saw the sharp, wary look entering Addams's eyes. "Yes, I'm related to *that* Cavanaugh," Duncan confirmed, then for emphasis, he spelled it out for the man. "Brian Cavanaugh. The chief of detectives."

Clearly intimidated, Addams responded like a cornered animal trying to make his enemy back off. "I don't take my orders from him," the man announced.

One way or another, the chief of detectives had a great deal of influence throughout all the departments. And they all knew it.

"You won't be taking orders from anyone pretty

soon if you keep this up," Duncan told him, keeping his statement just vague enough to allow Addams to put his own interpretation to what he'd just said.

Obviously that interpretation worked in their favor because, muttering disgruntled words under his breath, the coroner stormed over to the wall of metal doors and pulled open one of them that was located at approximately eye level.

"Here," he almost shouted, unzipping the black body bag and exposing the victim for viewing. "Satisfied?" he challenged.

"Getting there," Duncan replied mildly. "I believe Detective O'Banyon requested that you send the body over to the medical examiner's office."

"Sure, first chance I get," Addams retorted, turning away from the body. "Don't forget to close that when you're done," he groused as he stormed away.

The contents of the deceased's pockets, his wallet, a partial roll of breath mints and a key ring with several keys, were all tucked within a plastic zip bag and left laying on the man's blood-soaked chest.

Noelle quickly pulled on a set of rubber gloves she had in her pocket and opened the plastic bag. Gingerly, she took out the dead man's wallet and flipped it open to look at the license.

"Walter Teasdale," she read out loud, then murmured, "It's expired." Raising her eyes to her partner, she clarified her statement. "His license," she told Duncan, "it's expired."

The coroner's assistant continued to hover about

in the background, apparently doing his best to ignore his boss's exceedingly dark scowls.

"What was he doing out on the road, driving, then?" Silas innocently asked.

"Trying to beat the odds," Noelle concluded with more than a touch of sympathy. Checking the address, she placed the wallet back into the plastic bag. "He lived in the apartments not too far from where he crashed," she told Duncan. "Let's find out if he had any next of kin to notify." Turning toward the coroner, she asked, "Has that chance come up yet?"

Addams looked at her, irritated as well as confused. "Chance?"

"The first one you were supposed to use to get Mr. Teasdale here transported to the medical examiner's office."

The furrows in the coroner's brow deepened as he snapped, "No."

"I can do it," Silas offered, stepping forward and all but raising his hand as he volunteered. Taking note of the withering look his boss shot in his direction, the assistant seemed to almost fold into himself as he mumbled, "Or not."

Duncan flashed a reassuring smile at the man as he placed a hand on Silas's bony shoulder. "I'm sure my uncle will appreciate that," Duncan told him.

Still glaring, knowing when he'd lost, the coroner waved Silas on his way. "Go, cart the stiff off. One less body to account for," Addams muttered.

"You know, maybe you'd be happier in some other line of work," Noelle suggested to Addams crisply.

The expression in the man's dark brown eyes was nothing if not defiant. "No, I like dealing with dead people just fine. *They don't talk back,*" he emphasized, eyeing her pointedly. "It's the ones who aren't dead that I have trouble with."

Duncan tactfully moved his body in between Addams and his partner—just in case. He had no doubt that O'Banyon could only be pushed so far and no more. He was in essence saving Noelle from herself.

"This is just a guess," he told Addams, "but I think you just lost her vote for the Mr. Congeniality award." With that, he looked at Noelle. "You ready to go?" he asked.

"Oh, more than ready," she responded with feeling. Facing Addams, she said, "I'd like to thank you for all your help."

"Don't mention it," he retorted coldly.

Noelle pushed the swinging doors that led out of the coroner's quarters with both hands as she stormed out. She muttered something indiscernible under her breath.

Fury looked good on her, Duncan couldn't help thinking. But that didn't mean it was good *for* her or for the job.

"You know, part of being the lead on a case is learning not to let jerks like that get to you," he said as he hurried to keep up with Noelle. He had more

leg than she had, but keeping abreast of her took effort right now.

"So you wouldn't have wanted to strangle him?"
she challenged as she arrived at the elevator. She
punched the button a little harder than was war-
ranted.

"I didn't say that," he answered with a grin. "But
from his point of view, you invaded his little fiefdom
and challenged his authority. The guy was just lash-
ing out, trying to protect his territory."

In his own way, Cavanaugh had a point and she
knew it. Noelle shrugged, silently conceding the argument to her partner.

And then she thought of something that had
caught her attention earlier. "I thought you Cavanaughs never played the I've-got-relatives-in-high-
places card."

She knew that it was almost a point of honor with
them, each Cavanaugh insisting on making his or her
own way within the department without the help of
the rest of the family.

The elevator car finally arrived. Stepping in after
her, Duncan pressed the button for the first floor.
"They don't."

"But you do?" she questioned. The doors barely
closed and they were opening again, this time two
levels away on the first floor. Getting out, she headed
toward the rear of the building and the exit there.

"First time," Duncan admitted. "But Addams was
obviously a bully so I thought just this once, I could

be forgiven. Besides," he went on as he held the exit door open for her, "I didn't like the hard time he was giving you."

Walking out, she went down the cement steps and made her way toward their vehicle. "So that was why you decided to be my hero?"

"Your word, not mine," he said. "In my world, it takes a lot more to be a hero."

No, he'd tried to be her hero and normally, she would have balked at that. But not today. Not when it secretly felt so right—not that she would ever admit that to him as long as there was breath left in her body.

"Sometimes, the simplest acts leave the biggest impression," she told him. "But just so you know, I can take care of myself."

He had no doubt that she could, both verbally and physically if she had to. He'd seen her on the gun range. The woman was proficient. Watching her shoot was to watch a thing of beauty.

"Never said you couldn't," he replied. "And just so *you* know, this was more about Addams than about you. I've heard that you're not the first person he tried to browbeat and intimidate." Duncan looked at her over the dusty hood of the car. "Just the first one that I witnessed."

"So are you going to put him on report?" she asked.

"Not my usual style," Duncan admitted—but that didn't mean he couldn't turn over a new leaf. "But I haven't decided yet. People like that give the rest of the department a bad name. There're a lot of good people in the Crime Scene Investigative Unit—like Brenda."

Since he'd brought the woman's name up, she felt she could ask, "Speaking of whom, have you heard anything from her yet?"

"Not yet," he answered. "But she always makes a point of answering every question. Some answers just take longer," he added. He glanced down at the car and then at her. She was already on the driver's side, but she hadn't gotten in yet. "Do you want me to drive?" he offered.

"Thanks, but I'm fine, Cavanaugh. He didn't shake me up," she told him, guessing that Duncan probably thought that all this had gotten to her and sent her spiraling off into oblivion.

"Actually, I wasn't thinking that," he confessed to her.

Okay, he had her stumped now. "Then what *were* you thinking?"

"I thought that maybe, since you're the lead on this, you might like to be chauffeured around." He made the suggestion with a completely straight face.

She tried to ascertain whether or not Duncan was serious or just pulling her leg. Their relationship had evolved to this state, that he felt comfortable enough to tease her. She hadn't gotten to that place yet.

"What, no cushioned litter with four body servants carrying me to the apartment complex, à la Cleopatra?"

"I could call my brothers and see what we could arrange," he deadpanned.

Okay, he was kidding, she thought, relieved. "Thanks, but I'll just drive us there," she said, getting in behind the steering wheel. She put the key into the ignition.

"That works, too," he agreed.

Duncan had barely managed to get the seat belt's metal tongue into the slot when he felt her accelerating, pulling out of the parking lot and onto the road.

"Just a thought," he began as he watched Noelle merging the sedan into the right lane, then weaving into the next one because the cars were moving faster in that lane, "you might want to think about changing those shoes of yours."

She bit back the part about his not having any authority to tell her what and what not to wear on any part of her body.

Instead, she merely turned her head toward him for half a second and asked, "What?"

"Shoes," he repeated. "Get a pair with less lead in them," he suggested.

"Is that your clever way of saying I have a lead foot?" she asked him, barely having time to spare him a glance. The traffic was whizzing by almost as fast as she was.

"I don't know about 'clever,'" Duncan said cautiously, "but yeah, that's my way of saying you have a *really* lead foot. You do realize that getting there—wherever 'there' is—five minutes faster isn't going to matter if we're dead when we get there."

She didn't take kindly to lectures about her driving, no matter how discreetly the words were couched. At bottom a criticism was still a criticism.

"I've been driving like this since I got my license," Noelle informed her partner, hoping to get him to back away.

She should have known better.

"And I find that pretty scary." He paused, debating saying anything, then decided he had nothing to lose. "Did you ever consider the possibility that you might have used up all your luck by now?"

She glanced at him, and then, to his surprise, she eased back on the gas pedal. The car's speed lowered.

"You've decided you do have something to live for?" he asked her.

"Just didn't want to deprive your next date from enjoying the thrill of your company," she answered.

"I'll be sure to let her know about your thoughtfulness…once I figure out who she is," he added.

Chapter 10

There was no answer when they knocked on the door of Walter Teasdale's ground-floor apartment.

"He probably lived alone," Duncan guessed after he had knocked on the door for a second time with no results. "We might as well stop wasting time and just get the rental manager to let us into Teasdale's apartment," he told Noelle.

Noelle nodded. "I think we passed the office when we came into the complex. It's just in front of the pool area."

Duncan was already on his way to the rental office when she noticed that the door adjacent to the dead man's apartment was opened just a crack.

Just wide enough for her to see a pair of brown

eyes. Whoever they belonged to was apparently taking in everything going on in the common area between the two apartments.

Tapping Duncan's shoulder, she put her finger to her lips to keep him from saying anything when he turned around. She then silently pointed toward the other apartment.

Duncan spotted the eavesdropper for the first time and nodded. Walking up to the door, he addressed whoever was standing on the other side. "We're from the police department. Would you know if anyone else besides Walter Teasdale lives in 1F?"

The door didn't open any farther—but neither did it close. "How do I know you're from the police?" the person asked, a male by the sound of the challenging, reedy voice.

Duncan and his partner simultaneously took out their badges and IDs, flipping from one to the other and holding them up for the tenant to see.

"Detectives O'Banyon and Cavanaugh," Duncan announced, nodding first at Noelle and then indicating himself.

The door still didn't budge. "How do I know those aren't fakes?"

Duncan surprised Noelle by shrugging as he put his ID away and saying, "Guess you don't. Let's go, O'Banyon." With that he began to walk away.

She was about to voice a protest at his giving up so easily when the door of the adjacent apartment opened. She caught the smug look Duncan slanted in her direction before he turned around to face the resident in apartment 1E. She could almost hear Duncan's self-satisfied thoughts: he'd played a hunch and won. The tenant in 1E was far too curious to just let them walk away.

The tenant of 1E turned out to be an older, heavy-set, balding man whose main source of "exercise" appeared to be the hand-to-mouth variety, the kind involving bags of chips and fast foods, most likely delivered to his door.

Small, close-set brown eyes moved like syncopated marbles from one detective to the other and then back again.

"You're really the police?" he asked. Some of the suspicion was gone from his voice, replaced by eagerness. Whether that entailed a need for vicarious adventure or something else, Noelle wasn't sure yet. But she was optimistic.

"Yes, we're really the police," she assured the older man.

Before she could ask him anything, the tenant laughed almost gleefully. The deep scowl that had been on his face vanished completely.

"I knew it!" he cried triumphantly. "I knew it was too good to be true!" Interrupting his own revelry, the man told them, "He's not home. Walt's out celebrating, the poor jerk." The man was practically cackling now, laughing at some joke only he was privy to.

"Celebrating?" Duncan prodded, waiting to be enlightened.

"Celebrating what?" Noelle asked when the man didn't immediately reply.

The tenant held up his hand as he struggled to stop laughing and catch his breath. It took him more than a couple of minutes. Whatever the joke was, Noelle thought, it was apparently a good one in 1E's estimation.

"His so-called good fortune," the man answered. "He's been spending money like crazy since it happened."

So far, this wasn't making much sense. Noelle gave the man her most authoritative look, willing him to stop laughing long enough to let them in on what he deemed was so funny.

"Would you mind backing up a little for us, Mr.—" Pausing, she looked at the gleeful man, waiting for him to provide them with a name.

"Johnson," he told them, sucking in a gulp of air. "Jonas Johnson." His eyes were almost dancing as he asked, "Are you going to arrest him?"

Duncan exchanged glances with his partner. There was obviously something going on here that they were missing. He enunciated his question slowly. "Why would we want to arrest him?"

The question seemed to throw Johnson. "That's why you're here, isn't it? To arrest him. This thing can't be legal. I told Teasdale that. But would he listen? No, he would *not,*" Johnson declared with a triumphant air, then added like a man who had just been vindicated, "And now he's going to pay for that."

Maybe they were finally going to catch a break, Noelle thought. "You obviously seem to be in the know about what's going on here," she said to Johnson, playing up to the man's vanity.

"I am that," he confirmed proudly. "Walt acted all cocky and self-important about it. Said he was finally going to enjoy all the things he never had the opportunity to enjoy before. There's no such thing as a free lunch, right?" the balding man asked rhetorically, looking from Duncan to her, then back again, waiting for them to agree with him.

"Not as far as I know," Noelle replied.

"Why don't you tell us exactly what Walt thought was this so-called free lunch?" Duncan coaxed.

The deep-set brown marbles were on the move again, darting from one partner to the other as if to ascertain the trustworthiness of the two detectives standing on his doorstep.

"How much do you know?" the older man asked, looking from Duncan to her.

"Why don't you just pretend we don't know anything and fill us in on the whole thing?" Duncan suggested.

The man appeared more than ready to do just that. Gleefully. "Okay. About two years ago, this woman at the seniors' center, the one on Lake and East Yale Loop, not the other one," he qualified, since the city currently housed two seniors' centers. The one he was referring to was the newer of the two.

"Anyway, she said her name was Susan, and she approached Walt and said she had a proposition for him that he might find interesting. Well, Walt, he thought she meant *that* kind of a proposition—she had a real fantastic figure," he confided, winking at Duncan. "Well, right away, he tells her that he needed a little time to get his hands on the proper medication." Johnson paused for a moment to laugh at the memory. "She shoots down *that* air balloon pretty quick and tells him that her proposition involved helping him get a life insurance plan.

"At this point, Walt's real mad and he tells her he's not interested, that he's got nobody to leave the money to and he starts to walk away. She tells him that she knows all that, which stops him in his tracks. I mean, Walt's not famous or anything, so how does she know all this?" Johnson challenged.

On a roll, before either of them could comment, Johnson's voice took on steam. "She doesn't answer his question. Instead, she tells him that she was going to take care of all the details for him, pay all the premiums and give him a little something for his trouble, as well. *Then* she adds that if he lives for two years after the policy's issued without any incidents, she'll give him an extra fifty thousand dollars, kind of like a balloon payment with a mortgage, you know?" Johnson asked, looking to see if his audience was still with him.

Satisfied that they were, he continued. "The only thing she wanted Walt to do was to put down this so-called charitable foundation she worked for as the beneficiary of the policy—"

"What foundation?" Duncan asked. "Do you remember the name?"

"Not a clue," Johnson testified. And then he said, "Walt got that fifty-thousand-dollar check yesterday."

"You know that for a fact?" Noelle asked, studying Johnson's every move in an attempt to verify his narrative.

"Yeah, I know that for a fact," Johnson said in an annoyed tone. "Walt had the nerve to thumb his nose at me, laughed and said he was going to enjoy every penny of that money. That was the last time I saw him—taking off yesterday. Said something about buying a car, then looking that woman up. So, are you going to arrest him?" he asked eagerly, all but salivating at the very thought.

"I'm afraid we can't do that," Noelle replied solemnly.

Johnson was visibly disappointed—as well as angry. "Why not?" he demanded. "Why can't you arrest him? Is he missing?" He looked from one to the other again, searching for an answer. "Is that it? Is that why you were knocking on his door?"

"No, I'm afraid not," Noelle said, trying to find a way to soften the blow.

But Johnson wasn't about to be put off. "Then why won't you arrest him?"

"Because he's dead," Noelle finally told him.

Some of the other man's bravado and posturing faded. "Dead?" Johnson repeated, stunned. "What do you mean, 'dead'?"

"Dead," Duncan repeated with emphasis, then went on to elaborate, "As in not breathing. Permanently. Walter Teasdale ran his car into a tree. The coroner thinks he might have suffered a heart attack and lost control of the car."

"Heart attack?" Johnson echoed incredulously. His apparent confusion gave way to very real irritation. "Bull!"

"Why would you say that, Mr. Johnson?" Noelle asked, hoping that more than just jealousy was at play here.

"Walt had the heart of an athlete. He used to run until his knees gave out a couple of years back," Johnson recalled. "Hell, his doctor said he wished *his* heart was as healthy as Walt's was. Had to be something else," Johnson insisted, "'cause it couldn't have been his heart."

So much for the coroner's opinion, Noelle thought. "Well, Mr. Johnson, you've given us a lot to work with. If you think of something else, I'd appreciate it if you give me or my partner a call," she said, handing the tenant her card.

"Um, Detective O'Banyon?" Johnson called after her as she and Duncan began to walk away.

Turning, Noelle gave the man her full attention. "Yes?"

"Did Walt have any money left on him when you found him?" Johnson ventured out of the doorway of his apartment. "I mean, he's got nobody and I'm the closest to a family member he had. I just thought, if there was any of that fifty thousand left, I could maybe use it for his funeral expenses," he added as an afterthought, apparently thinking that might do the trick.

"We didn't find any money on him," Duncan told him, sparing her the trouble of answering. "But we can check with the coroner's office in case we missed something."

A definite ray of hope entered Johnson's eyes. "Let me know," he said just before he closed his door.

She looked at Duncan as they walked to the complex's rental office. They still had to rummage through the victim's apartment for some clue that might lead them to the woman who had convinced Teasdale to take out the life insurance policy.

Noelle's mind, however, was on something her partner had just said. "You think that someone in the coroner's office took the man's stash?"

Duncan shook his head. That answer had strictly been for Johnson's benefit, to keep him available to them in case there were further questions. "No. I think that this mysterious woman might have decided that Walt would have no further use for the money and *she* took it."

That sounded far more plausible to her. "Before or after the accident?"

"My guess would be just before, but I'm not married to the idea, so if you have any thoughts on the matter, I'm open to them," he told her gamely.

"Let's see what we can find in his apartment first," she said hopefully.

"Well," Duncan said less than ten minutes later as he and Noelle surveyed Teasdale's apartment— or what was left of it, "if there *was* anything to be found here, it's most likely gone now."

The apartment the rental manager had unlocked for them had been completely tossed. Nothing was left standing or resting in its original place.

Even so, it appeared to be an apartment at odds with itself.

For the most part, Teasdale's small one-bedroom apartment appeared almost Spartan in its decor— which was now scattered about on the floor. Spartan except for the huge fifty-inch high-definition flat screen TV mounted on the wall, the expensive bottle of red wine Duncan discovered in the refrigerator and the several state-of-the-art electronic devices that were thrown about the eight-hundred-square-foot apartment.

"You see a cell phone around here?" Duncan asked, turning toward her.

She'd chosen that exact same moment to come up behind him. As a result, his body brushed against hers and even though she quickly moved back, the flash of electricity had more than registered with her. With him as well, she realized by the expression on his face. She felt desire urging her on. That she managed to shut it away was a testimony of her inner strength—and a cause for inner frustration as well.

"No," she managed to say after a shaky moment. "And there wasn't one in the plastic bag that was left with his body, either," she recalled.

Pretending as if he hadn't just endured a blast of heat, Duncan nodded. "It doesn't seem logical, given these other toys, that the man wouldn't have a cell phone. A smartphone is a 'must have' for anyone who's into electronic toys. My guess is that it could have been thrown from the car," he theorized.

That might have been his "guess," but Cavanaugh certainly didn't sound convinced, she couldn't help thinking.

"But you don't really think so, do you?" Noelle said out loud.

He didn't and he told her why. "That cell might have had that woman's number on it," he said. "If she's smart enough to come up with this scheme, then she's smart enough to want to get rid of the evidence."

Taking out his own cell phone, Duncan punched in a number on the keypad. When he saw the silent question in his partner's eyes, he said, "I think that CSI will want to take a look at this place, see what they make of it and whose prints they might be able to unearth." And then he grinned at her. "Congratulations, O'Banyon."

Well, that had certainly come out of the blue, she thought. "For what?"

"I told you to go with your instincts. Looks like your instincts were dead-on—no pun intended," he added. The next moment, he snapped to attention as a voice came on the line.

Noelle thought of the crumpled body she had seen on the side of the road and knew that she wished she'd been wrong.

"I didn't know you'd switched over to Homicide," Sean Cavanaugh, the head of Aurora's CSI day shift, said to Duncan when he arrived on the scene with his crew some twenty minutes later.

"I didn't," Duncan told the man. "I'm still in Vice. This investigation came about because of my partner." He nodded toward Noelle in case there were any doubts.

Recognition came in an instant. Sean's customary, amicable smile instantly turned personal. "Oh, yes, you're the one whose grandmother kept Shamus enthralled all evening," he said with a soft laugh, referring to the father he had recently been reunited with. "I haven't seen my father that happy looking since I first met him," he added.

The statement served only to confuse Noelle even further.

Since he was her guide through all things Cavanaugh, she looked to Duncan for an explanation.

An explanation that was not about to be forthcoming any time soon.

"Long story," Duncan murmured. "I'll tell it to you some time over drinks."

"That's a deal I'm going to hold you to," she warned Duncan, putting him on notice before turning back to Sean and the crew that he had brought with him. CSI needed to be filled in on the little information that they actually had at their disposal.

Once that was done, she and Duncan were about to go back to the precinct when Noelle had an idea. It was probably nothing more than a desperate shot in the dark, but it might be worth a try.

Instead of getting back into the white sedan, Noelle went to Johnson's door and knocked. "Mr. Johnson, it's Detectives O'Banyon and Cavanaugh again. Could we please have another word with you?"

The door flew open almost immediately.

It was obvious that what was going on in the apartment next door was the most excitement Johnson had seen in a very long time. He clearly wanted to be a part of it as much as humanly possible.

"Sure, what word would you want to use?" he asked, laughing at his own display of humor.

"If we put you together with a sketch artist at our precinct, do you think you might be able to describe the woman who approached your friend at the seniors' center? I know it's been a while," Noelle apologized, trying to give him a way out if he didn't recall the person's features. "But—"

"You don't forget someone who makes your best friend rich," Johnson told them solemnly.

Apparently Walter Teasdale's status had been upgraded in the past hour, Noelle thought, going from being just an acquaintance to suddenly being referred to as a "best friend." She couldn't help wondering what the dead man would be to Johnson by tomorrow morning.

"Or a woman with such a firm butt like that one," Johnson added, ruining the moment. From the look on his face, the neighbor was visualizing the woman he was referring to.

"So you have no problem coming to the station with us?" she asked, wanting to be perfectly clear on the subject. They needed a sketch of this woman just in case she had done more than just feed the fantasies of an old man and inadvertently brought about his death prematurely.

"No problem at all," Johnson answered, sounding positively cheerful about the prospect of coming down to the precinct to tell a sketch artist what he remembered.

"Just let me change my shoes," he added for her benefit. "Can't go to the police station wearing slippers."

Johnson was whistling something uplifting and cheerful as he went to find his shoes.

"Wonder if this is going to turn out to be a wild-goose chase," Duncan speculated, whispering to his partner.

"Well, at least we've got a wild goose to chase. That's more than we had a few minutes ago," she pointed out.

He glanced at her, a grin she couldn't begin to interpret on his lips. "O'Banyon, you surprise me. Under all that darkness, you really are an optimist, aren't you?"

"I just like keeping my options open, that's all," she told him.

Anything he might have to say to counter or comment on that had to wait. Johnson reappeared in the doorway and brightly announced, "Okay, got my shoes on. All set. Let's go."

"You heard the man," Noelle said to her partner. "Let's go."

Chapter 11

"Y̲ou're just going to draw her head?" Jonas Johnson asked incredulously more than an hour later as the sketch artist turned the monitor toward him, displaying a completed version of the woman Johnson had described as the one who had talked his neighbor into buying a life insurance policy. All the specific nuances that the fussy old man had recalled had been taken into account.

However, it was apparent that Johnson felt her most important feature was being ignored.

"Yes," Alan Kwan replied. Chosen for this particular position not just because of his ability to conceptualize random features and descriptions, turning them into realistic renditions of a whole, but for his inordinate patience, as well, Alan looked at the man who had become a definite challenge to the latter quality. "What's wrong? Doesn't it look like her?"

"Well, yeah," Johnson allowed, shrugging his sloping shoulders haplessly, "but you're not showing her best features. Trust me, if you expect people to recognize her, you should at least draw some more of her."

"More?" Noelle asked, coming over to check on the progress that had been made. She glimpsed the exasperated look on Alan's face before he looked her way. She felt for the man.

Johnson, sitting in the chair beside Alan's desk, turned now to face her.

"Well, yeah," he answered as if any fool could see what he was talking about. "The woman had a chest that could make you just fall to your knees because they got so weak. Well, maybe not you," he amended.

"Thank you for that," she murmured under her breath. "Sketches are usually of just the person's head," she told Teasdale's neighbor.

Johnson shook his head adamantly. "But if you're gonna show that around, I guarantee that the guys who'll remember her ain't gonna remember her face, not without that—other part of her in the sketch." He chose his words more carefully because he was talking to a woman.

"Thanks. We'll keep that in mind," Noelle told him. She'd overheard what Johnson had said to the sketch artist and there was no way she was going to pass around a sketch of a woman with a pronounced glandular problem. *Someone* had to recognize her face. "Alan, would you mind getting one of the uniforms to bring Mr. Johnson back to his apartment again?"

Alan seemed more than ready to have the whiny old man taken off his hands. "You got it," he agreed, a genuine, wide smile on his face.

"I don't have to go right away," Johnson protested. "I thought I could hang around here for a while, until you brought that woman in. You know, do a personal ID, that kind of stuff."

"I'm afraid that that sort of thing might take a while, Mr. Johnson. I have your number. We can give you a call if we need you," she assured him, then turned toward the sketch artist. "Alan, that ride…?" She let her voice trail off, thinking that the hopeful note in it was enough to tip the man off that he wasn't the only one who *really* wanted Johnson taken home ASAP.

"Right." Alan tucked his arm through Johnson's, gently but firmly urging the man to his feet. "C'mon, Mr. Johnson, let's see if we can get you home."

Johnson's head all but did a one-eighty as he tried to keep her in view. "You sure?" he asked, the sorrowful look on his face making him appear every bit like a lost puppy hoping to be adopted.

"We're sure, Mr. Johnson," Noelle replied firmly.

A huge sigh filled the squad room as Johnson reluctantly allowed himself to be led away.

"You have a groupie?" Duncan asked, coming over to the sketch artist's area to find out what was keeping her. He'd been just in time to catch the end of the exchange between Johnson and his partner.

She watched as Alan, holding firmly on to Johnson, disappeared outside the hallway. "What I have," she told Duncan as she turned around to face him, "is a pain in the neck."

He glanced toward the sketch on the monitor before giving his attention to Noelle. "There are remedies for that," he teased, his mouth curving just the slightest bit.

Noelle deliberately avoided his eyes, looking at the sketch instead. "Thanks, but I'll tough it out," she said.

Somehow, to her irritation, her partner seemed to fill the entire area around her, despite the fact that there were other people in the squad room with at least half a dozen conversations going back and forth at any given time.

"Nothing wrong with being soft once in a while," Duncan commented easily, his voice annoyingly low and, if she didn't know any better, sensual.

"Sure there is," she said with conviction. "If you're 'soft,' you get stepped on and trampled all the time."

He was not about to get sucked into an argument about that. Instead, he pointed out what he felt was the obvious. "That was before you had me watching your back.

She looked at him for a long-drawn-out moment. "It's usually the person closest to you who *is* in the best position to do the trampling." *Okay, enough, time to get back to business,* she told herself. Noelle gestured toward the monitor. "Let's get copies of this passed around. Maybe we'll get lucky and somebody'll recognize this woman."

Noelle frowned without realizing it as she examined the sketch. Maybe it was her imagination, but just for a moment, the woman looked vaguely familiar. She was sure that a lot of people would probably think the same thing. The woman had that sort of a face.

Even if someone *did* recognize the woman, it could just lead them to another dead end. This was a long shot at best, but at the moment, they didn't have anything else.

Duncan took a closer look at the sketch on the monitor. "Nothing very remarkable about her to set her apart," he commented, then predicted, "this is going to be an uphill battle." He saw his partner's lips curve a little. "What?"

"I'm told she has a remarkable set of...breathing apparatuses," she replied.

Duncan laughed. The sound seemed to ripple right through her. "Might make an interesting footnote to work into the description," he mused.

Something he said triggered a thought. Rather than share it with him, Noelle turned on her heel and hurried back to her desk without a word.

Seeing her dash off like that aroused his curiosity and he followed her back to their desks. "Hey, was it something I said?"

The question was without a trace of humor in it, but with Duncan, she was beginning to realize it was hard to tell when he was being serious and when he was kidding. She decided to treat it as if it was the former.

Which was why she surprised him by looking over her shoulder and saying, "Yes."

Although he had no idea what he might have said to suddenly get the wheels in her head turning and have her all but fly across the squad room to her desk—more specifically, to her computer—he did smile to himself as a feeling of satisfaction took hold. Whatever else was going on around them and between them, he and O'Banyon were beginning to gel as a team. The kind that eventually finished each other's sentences as well as each other's thoughts.

The kind, he added silently, who solved crimes.

The only other time he'd encountered that sort of thing—from the outside—was between two people in a relationship. The kind that eventually heated up and either burned the people involved—or warmed them. He had an itch to find out which they would wind up being.

But that would be after this case was over, not now, he told himself.

The problem was, he really wasn't listening to his own words of so-called wisdom.

"What is it that's going through your head?" he asked when he reached his desk. For the time being, he remained standing, just in case she wanted him looking over her shoulder—literally—at something.

"Obituaries," she said without looking up.

Okay, he'd bite. "Why obituaries? You're kind of young to be obsessing about the obituary page, don't you think?" he asked.

"Not obsessed," she said, sparing him a glance to help underscore the difference, "just homing in."

He wasn't about to drop the subject until she gave him an answer he could work with. "On?"

Her fingers flew across the keyboard as she pulled up issues of the largest local paper in the county. This was her starting point, she decided. There was always time to expand to other newspapers.

Duncan and his questions were almost a distraction right now. "On how many people, say fifty and older, were not survived by any loved ones."

Since she had obviously connected the dots, he put the question to her rather than trying to puzzle it out for himself. He saw no advantage to coming to his own conclusion instead of just using hers. Most likely, it would be the same. "Just where are you going with this, O'Banyon?"

"Just a hunch," she told him, typing. "More like a thought, really." She scrolled down a screen that appeared, and then another. "Or—"

"O'Banyon, stop looking for adjectives and just spit it out."

She stopped typing. "What if this is the tip of the iceberg?"

"What kind of iceberg?" he asked.

There were so many ways this could be bad for the victims involved, she wasn't sure just where to begin.

"A deadly scam," she finally said. "What if someone's getting older people to buy life insurance polices, paying them to take out the policies on themselves, plus putting up the money for the premiums—"

So far, he thought, she was just rephrasing what Johnson had told them about Teasdale. Before he could say so, she added what had her worried.

"—and then, when enough time has passed, they terminate the old person in order to collect on their policies sooner than later. Think about it," she said, growing excited as the idea took on form for her. "If these people have no next of kin, or anyone they're close to, who's to get suspicious if they suddenly pass away? Old people die, it's just the way things are, just like you said," she concluded matter-of-factly. "So nobody looks into it."

"You're thinking of Lucy's friends, aren't you? Sally and Henry," he supplied.

"It wouldn't hurt to check it out," Noelle said.

"It never hurts to check things out," he agreed, "but didn't you say that Lucy told you the money went to some foundation or charity?"

"Yes, but how do we know these organizations are legitimate? Doesn't take much to set up shop and declare yourself a nonprofit organization dedicated to protecting fireflies from extinction by natural predators."

Hell of a mouthful, he thought.

Hell of a mouth.

The thought came out of nowhere, both surprising him and maybe unsettling him slightly, as well. He liked to be on top of things, initiate them, not find himself being dragged in by a stray thought or feeling. That sort of thing took control out of his hands. And he had always been about control. This woman, though, this petite, driven firecracker, by her sheer existence in his life, was changing all the rules on him. And damn, but he was letting it happen.

That wasn't like him.

Duncan sought refuge in humor until he could sort things out a little.

"Now that you mention it, there are no fireflies out here," he deadpanned.

She shot him an impatient glance. "You know what I mean."

"Yeah, I do," he said with a laugh before growing serious again. "And you might have a point," he agreed. "Or," he felt obligated to mention, "this could all be just one giant coincidence and despite some popular beliefs to the contrary, sometimes coincidences actually *do* happen."

"But what if it's not?" she challenged. "What if it's *not* a coincidence? Maybe it started out innocent enough, but whoever's behind this decided that the old people weren't dying fast enough to supply them with the money they needed? What if there's someone out there, or more than just one someone, capitalizing on the fact that most people are trusting and doing away with old people for their own gain?"

Duncan sat down at his own desk and turned his attention to his computer, pulling up the obituary section of another county newspaper. "Then I guess we'd better get busy," he murmured.

By the end of what was left that day, they had come up with six obituaries that filled the basic requirements Noelle had thought of. Six senior citizens in or around Aurora who had died in the past six months and whose obituaries omitted mentioning any surviving family members.

She saw the frown on Duncan's face. Was he just tired, or had he thought of something? Incredibly tired herself, rather than frame a question, Noelle merely asked him, "What?"

Duncan raised his eyes to hers. "If there *are* no surviving family members and the deceased isn't some person important to the company or community, then who's the obituary for?" he asked.

That hadn't occurred to her. "Good question," Noelle acknowledged, thinking. "Maybe it's some sort of signal to let another person in on this scam know that they're cashing in on another policy."

He nodded. That was one explanation. "Or maybe it's just more proof to the insurance company that's going to be paying out on this policy that the person died."

"There still has to be a death certificate produced in order to get the policy benefit," she told him.

"Yeah, but just think of the obituary as being the bow on a package."

Noelle let that go for now. She found the whole thing immensely disturbing, especially since the victims she was looking at were listed as being all around her grandmother's age.

"So how do you think they do it," she asked him, "these people who are getting these senior citizens to buy policies?"

"They bribe them, like Johnson said that woman bribed Teasdale into getting a policy."

She wasn't talking about the mechanics, she was referring to the actual murders. "No, I mean how do you think these people are eliminating the victims? With poison, or—?"

"Hell, there are lots of way to kill someone," he said. As a Cavanaugh, with as many members of his family on the police force as there were, he'd heard scores of unusual, disturbing stories. "Accidents happen all the time. Heart attacks can be simulated. A lot of times they say that a person died in his or her sleep from natural causes." He looked at her. "Maybe those causes weren't really so natural."

"We need an autopsy," she concluded. An autopsy would give them proof if drugs were used to cause these people's hearts to stop. "Speaking of which, when are we going to hear the result of Teasdale's autopsy?"

Duncan laughed shortly. He didn't want to dampen her enthusiasm, but she needed to be aware of the truth. "Not for a while, I'm guessing. Contrary to what they show you on all those crime shows on TV, it takes a while to get any kind of real results to the tests that have to be performed."

"Why?"

"Most of the time, the medical examiner is backed up. He doesn't just handle Aurora but the surrounding cities, as well. We have to wait our turn," he told her, then added, "and I've got this feeling that the coroner is going to take his sweet time getting Teasdale's body transported. And who knows how many bodies the M.E. has right now that are ahead of ours, so—"

She stopped him before he could continue. "Can't you do something about it?"

The question caught him off guard. "I'm afraid I never got a do-it-yourself autopsy kit for Christmas as a kid, so no, much as I might want to, I can't do something about it."

She frowned at Cavanaugh. The man knew perfectly well what she was referring to. She spelled it out for him. "I mean, can't you use your influence? Like throw your weight around as a Cavanaugh to get them to speed things up, something like that?"

If anything, he would have bet money that she was a straight arrow who *always* played by the rules as they were written. This was an intriguing side to her he hadn't expected. "What?"

"You did it with the coroner—" Noelle reminded him.

"That was a one-time thing," he explained, "and I did it mainly because I didn't like the way the coroner was talking down to you. I wanted to put him in his place because he deserved it. However, around my house, it was always kind of an unspoken rule that we *didn't* throw our weight around."

So he did have principles. Who knew? "Sorry, didn't mean to cross any lines," she apologized. Her frustration was getting the better of her, she realized. If she'd been thinking clearly, she wouldn't have suggested that.

This was more like her, he thought. Right now, he wasn't altogether sure which Noelle he found more appealing, the straight arrow or the one who liked having the rules bent.

"That's okay… Of course," he went on, thinking out loud, "there's no law that I can't talk to Uncle Sean—the head of the CSI day shift—" he tossed in, in case she wasn't aware of that "—to maybe talk to the M.E. and see if things can't be nudged along." Even as he said it, he was picking up the phone on his desk.

She smiled. "I knew you were good for something."

He looked at her significantly as the phone on the

other end of the line was ringing. "Oh, O'Banyon, you have no idea the things I'm good for."

It was a joke, a throwaway line that was said and forgotten the next moment, she silently insisted. Why it would create a warm shiver up and down her spine she had absolutely no idea—and no time—to explore either her reaction or the possibilities Cavanaugh was so sensually alluding to. No time at all. Another senior citizen's life might be coldly and cruelly cut short if she and Cavanaugh didn't get to the bottom of this, and soon.

"Why don't you call it a day and we can get an early start tomorrow?" Duncan suggested the next day at very close to the same time they had simultaneously burned out the night before.

Their shift had ended half an hour ago and they were both still at their desks, still poring over details and news clippings on the internet, trying to find something that might point them in the right direction.

Her eyes were blurry as she stared at the computer monitor. She needed eye drops. "Just another five minutes."

"That's what you said half an hour ago," he told her. The woman needed a keeper. "You're getting punchy. Go home to your little girl. Get some sleep."

"Spoken like a man who never had a little girl— or little boy—in his life. *Sleep* and *children* do not belong in the same sentence," she informed him in a voice that echoed of fatigue.

"Okay, ask Lucy to babysit while you catch up on your sleep. We can look at this with fresh eyes tomorrow." He had a feeling that they would have been further ahead in all this if Brenda had managed to get back to them with her findings, but in true Murphy's Law fashion, Brenda had come down with a really bad case of the flu and was out of commission for now.

"I'm fresh," she insisted.

Walking around to her side of the desk, he pushed the keyboard away from her fingers and pulled back the chair she was sitting on. "Far be it from me to contradict a lady, but you're not fresh, you're wilting."

"Look, I should know whether I'm fresh or not." Even as she said it, she told herself she was going to argue with Duncan for maybe one more round before giving up and going home. Her stubborn streak just didn't want him to win easily. "Look, Cavanaugh, you can go home if you want, but I'm—"

"Detective Cavanaugh, I've got an autopsy report for you, care of CSI supervisor Sean Cavanaugh," a uniformed policeman announced, putting a long manila envelope on his desk.

Her exhaustion abruptly vanishing, Noelle was on her feet in an instant, rounding her desk and his until she laid hands on the envelope and held it up to him

"Open it, open it," she cried.

Taking it from her, he was visibly amused as he unsealed the flap.

"What do you think I was going to do with this, have it bronzed?" Duncan asked her, slipping the report out of the envelope.

They saw it together, homing in on it as if there were a spotlight shining on the one line that could torpedo the budding investigation.

The line that said that Teasdale appeared to have died from a heart attack, and that the heart attack subsequently went on to be the cause of his losing control of the vehicle he was driving, ultimately crashing into the tree.

Noelle blew out a breath as for one brief moment, her stomach fell about as far as physically and emotionally possible.

Chapter 12

The next minute, Noelle rallied and snapped out of her momentary funk. "That doesn't prove anything," she declared.

To her surprise, Duncan agreed with her.

"You're right, it doesn't." Quickly, he glanced over the rest of the preliminary autopsy information. "There is an outside chance the situation was manipulated. There're drugs that can simulate a heart attack once they're in your system. If Teasdale was somehow injected just before he drove off, or more likely, if he unknowingly ingested a drug that could mimic the symptoms of a heart attack, he'd wind up crashing just the way he did and it would look like an unfortunate accident caused by a heart attack." He went further with his theory. "If there are any witnesses to the accident or if it was caught on a traffic camera, I'd bet that Teasdale was seen clutching at his chest."

Which meant that they were still looking at murder, she thought. "So what we need is to have a full-on tox screen performed."

Duncan nodded. "And that's going to take some time—even with weight thrown around," he added, anticipating her next suggestion.

She knew that. Knew that tox screen results didn't just materialize on a page with the wave of a magic wand. Unable to bear the idea of just idly standing around, waiting on lab results, she switched her focus. "I guess we need another body."

Duncan looked at her. Was she saying what he thought she was saying? That sounded rather cold and the woman he was getting to know behind all those barriers was not cold or unfeeling. Still, he had to clarify what she was saying for himself. "You mean another old person supposedly dropping dead under suspicious circumstances?"

Noelle shook her head. She was fervently hoping that there had been a temporary moratorium declared on dead senior policy holders to avoid further deaths. However, she knew how greedy some people could be and how they felt themselves invulnerable. More than likely, the deaths would continue.

"No, a *body*," she stressed. "One that's already

dead. We need to exhume one of the people we found in those obituaries we pulled up."

"Not exactly easy," Duncan pointed out. "It's not like taking a shovel and pail to the beach. We need to get either a court order or permission from next of kin—and these people *have* no next of kin. That's the whole point."

She wasn't comfortable admitting that there were areas in her law enforcement education that still needed filling in. "How should we go about getting a court order?" she asked.

To her relief, her partner didn't take the opportunity to ridicule her lack of knowledge—and he could have, given his background. Cavanaugh was turning out to be a really nice guy.

"We have to show probable cause," Duncan answered. "And a hunch doesn't qualify if that's what you're going to suggest."

"Actually," she said out loud, "I *wasn't* going to say that. I was just going to recall that at your brother's wedding, I thought I heard someone call one of the guests 'Judge,'" she told him. "If he's a friend of the family—"

It had taken him a while to get everyone straight in this new branch of the family that had been accidentally uncovered a little more than a year ago, getting names, faces and in some cases, careers down pat. Not everyone was as obsessive as he was, but despite his laid-back manner, Duncan liked keeping things straight. It gave him a sense of order.

"Actually," he corrected, "there are two judges *in* the family itself."

Her eyes lit up and the sight all but mesmerized him for a moment. They had to be the brightest shade of green he'd ever seen.

"Great," she exclaimed.

"Not so great," he contradicted. "This isn't like having an inside track on something. If anything, it makes things a little more difficult. We still have to show probable cause, even with one of our own. Probably *more* so with our own so that the actions— or results—aren't held suspect.

"You know," he said, thinking it over slowly, "We might have an easier time of it with either one of those friends of your grandmother."

"You mean Sally and Henry?" When he nodded in response, she had her doubts about the wisdom of his suggestion. "Why should it be easier? She wasn't related to either one of them."

There were times when extenuating circumstances could be taken into consideration. "But she was a close friend to them, right?"

"Right," Noelle agreed. "I think Lucy was most likely Henry's *only* friend," she speculated, remembering. "If his funeral was anything to go on."

He was trying to pull together all the information he could that might be useful to make their case. "She paid for that, didn't she?"

"Technically." When he gave her a puzzled look, she explained, "From what I gathered, Henry had set some money aside to cover the funeral expenses. He did give Lucy access to the account."

"So *technically*," he emphasized, "Lucy was the executor of Henry's estate, right?" Duncan was fishing for the right wording that would allow them to pursue this autopsy.

Noelle eyed her partner as the light suddenly went off in her head. Why hadn't *she* considered that? Maybe she was more tired than she thought.

"Right," she agreed.

"Okay," he said, "first thing in the morning, we see about the proper steps to be taken to get the exhumation process started."

She saw him turning off his computer. "Why not now?" she protested.

"Because," he explained patiently, "the powers that be who can sign off on these things like to get their beauty sleep, which I suggest we do, as well." Pushing his desk drawer closed, he paused to glance in her direction. "Although you don't need any help in that department from where I'm standing."

As she closed down her own computer, it took her a second to play back his words and make sense of them. "Was that a compliment?"

Duncan laughed shortly. "If you have to ask, then either it didn't come out very well or you're more tired than either one of us thinks."

"It wouldn't work, you know," Noelle told him as she stopped to double-check if she had everything she wanted to take with her. Satisfied, she pushed her chair into her desk.

The comment had come out of left field and he wasn't sure just what his partner was talking about. "*What* wouldn't work?"

Turning, she began to head for the hall. "Something between us," Noelle answered. She nodded at one of the few remaining detectives in the squad room as she passed his desk. "It wouldn't work."

Duncan caught up to her in two strides, crossing the threshold a half step behind her only because he didn't want to crowd her. "What makes you say that?"

She frowned as she kept her eyes straight ahead and walked to the elevators. "Because I'm the Black Queen."

"I think the term you're looking for is Black Widow, not Black Queen." He laughed at the mistake only because of the strange image the latter title conjured up in his head. Something out of a feature-length cartoon he'd seen as a kid. "Man, you really are punchy, aren't you?"

"Maybe." She punched the down button extra hard. "But that doesn't mean I'm wrong. Unless, of course," she threw out offhand, "you have a death wish."

"Not a death wish," he corrected, then did own up to a quirk he possessed, "but I do like to live life on the edge."

The elevator arrived and she stepped in. Because

of the hour, the shift change had already taken place and they were alone in the small car. "And working in Vice with a side order of homicide isn't enough 'edginess' for you?"

Reaching around her, his arm brushing against the side of her arm, he pressed the first-floor button. "I like to leave myself open to having new experiences." Arriving at the first floor, he let her step out first as the doors opened. "Hey, you feel like stopping at Malone's for a beer?" he suggested.

She'd been to the establishment regarded as a cop bar only twice: once as a uniformed police officer and once when she'd received her promotion. For the most part, after a full day, all she wanted to do was seek out the comfort of her home and her small family. But she knew of others who made a point to stop at Malone's every night after their shift just to unwind before going home.

"Are you trying to ply me with liquor?" she deadpanned.

He laughed. "One beer is not *plying*."

"Okay, how many beers does it take to qualify for plying?" she asked as they walked down the hallway to the back exit.

He thought for a moment. "At least four if your tolerance is low."

"Let's say it is, then what happens?" she asked.

At the door, he pushed it opened and then held it for her. "Then I can't let you drive. I'd have to drive you home."

Walking out, she turned toward him. The wind had picked up and rippled through her hair, causing strands to playfully glide along his face. "Whose home?"

For the slightest second, he felt his stomach tighten. Duncan sternly reminded himself that she was his partner, not his date. The thought seemed to get lost in translation.

"Whoever's home you want it to be," he answered significantly.

Noelle made no comment on that, didn't really trust herself to at the moment. Instead, she asked, "And if the reverse happens?"

"You mean you plying me?" he asked, surprised that she would pose the question. Further surprised when she nodded in response. "That's easy. Then I'd count on you driving *me* home."

She stopped on the bottom step of the building before heading toward her car in the parking lot. "Same question."

His mouth slowly curved, the impression all the more sensual looking for its speed. "Same answer," he countered.

She took a breath, made her decision and dove in. "Okay."

He was unclear as to what she had just agreed to. "Okay what?"

Noelle unconsciously wet her lips before replying. "Okay, let's go to Malone's for that beer and see what happens."

Surprised and momentarily taken aback, it took Duncan a second to get moving.

Noelle slowly looked around as she followed Duncan into Malone's, taking in the atmosphere. It appeared to be more crowded tonight than it had the other two times she'd been here.

The din seemed to envelop her the moment she crossed the threshold, but rather than be the source of stress or annoyance, the din was somehow warm and soothing rather than jarring.

They were making their way toward the bar and she found she had to lean in to Duncan to make herself heard. "If I were a civilian, I'd feel very safe in here," she told him. "The place has wall-to-wall cops. The last time I saw so many cops was at your brother's wedding."

He glanced around as he continued to forge a path for them to the bar to place their order.

"Actually—" Duncan hazarded a guess "—I think there were more there than here, but I might be wrong." Arriving at the bar, he turned to her as he signaled for the bartender. "So, beer?" he asked, double-checking.

She'd never cared for the bitter taste. Noelle shook her head. "Club soda."

Duncan arched one eyebrow in amusement. "So, I take it that you've changed your mind about seeing what happens?"

"Just saving you from disaster," she said matter-of-factly. "I've decided that I like having you as a partner and I really don't want death to be entering that equation."

He looked at her for a long moment before saying, "I thought it already had." The bartender had reached them at this point, so Duncan gave the man their order. "Scotch on the rocks and one club soda for the lady."

"Not someone else's death," she corrected as the bartender moved to the side to retrieve a bottle of Scotch. "Yours."

Returning, the bartender poured the dark amber liquid over the ice in the glass. "You really do believe in that stuff, don't you?" Duncan asked.

"Doesn't have anything to do with believing or not believing. It happened," she answered matter-of-factly. She nodded at the bartender as the latter partially emptied an individual-size bottle of club soda into a glass and moved that in front of her. "I buried two fiancés," Noelle added solemnly.

Duncan paused to take one sip of his drink, then looked at her thoughtfully. "So I'll be okay as long as we don't get engaged."

Because of the swelling noise level in the bar, he was forced to repeat the words into her ear in order for her to hear him.

A warm shiver, generated by his breath along her skin, had her reacting in ways she didn't welcome. Ways that seemed to seep into her soul with an intensity that took her breath away.

She closed her eyes for a second, pushing the sensation back and getting a tight rein over herself. Or trying to.

"Right," she murmured, forcing the word out since her mouth had decided to suddenly go very dry, causing the words to stick to her tongue. "No engagement."

Glass in hand, he smiled over the rim. The smile went directly into her chest. "Problem solved."

"No," she contradicted strongly, or thought she did, "problem just started."

They remained at Malone's for the better part of half an hour, interacting with members of the force, trading pleasantries and trying to pretend that the work they did had obligingly remained at the threshold when they had entered the establishment.

But the evening was getting on and eventually they began to make their way back to the entrance.

The outside world hit them with a blast of cool night air, made cooler still by the contrast of the atmosphere inside the bar and outside of it.

"Looks like you won't be needing that ride home," he commented, referring to her very sober state.

"How about you?" she asked.

He laughed shortly at the question. "If one drink could render me incapable of driving, then I'm in big trouble."

She slowly shook her head. "No, I mean why don't you come home with me?"

He looked at her for a long moment, wondering if she actually knew what she was saying—wondering if *he* knew for that matter. "Sure."

"We can talk to Lucy together about getting her to okay Henry's exhumation."

He upbraided himself for allowing his imagination to run off and get the better of him. What else could she have meant except for that? The woman was as straitlaced as the day was long. "Oh. You want me to talk to Lucy."

And then, stopping by her vehicle and turning around to face him, she said something that blew everything else sky-high. "After she goes home, you can talk to me—if you want."

Their eyes met and held for a moment as he tried to tell himself that his imagination was running away with him again. They definitely could *not* be on the same page—could they?

He would have doubted it, doubted there was anything but the most innocent of statements behind her words. But the expression he caught in her eyes had him thinking that maybe, just maybe, he needed to reexamine his conclusions and the evidence one more time.

He let his breath out slowly, sounding very much in control of himself and the moment.

"Sounds like a plan to me," he said. "I'll follow

you home," he offered, then added for good measure, "To talk to Lucy."

Her smile was not just compelling, it was also enigmatic. He had never felt quite this confused before.

Lucy looked from her granddaughter to Duncan. Melinda was upstairs, asleep, and they had succinctly placed their idea before her, waiting for her response.

"I can do that? I can request an autopsy after the fact?" Lucy asked, digesting what Duncan and her granddaughter had told her.

"Yes," Duncan answered.

"But I wasn't Henry's next of kin," Lucy protested.

"Doesn't matter," he assured her. "You're the executor of his estate."

"What estate?" she asked dismissively. "Henry left seven thousand in a savings certificate for his funeral expenses. The other money, that big payoff from the insurance policy, I found out that's going to some charity he got talked into," she said with a shrug of her shoulders, then looked at her granddaughter. "Do you know if the charity is legitimate?"

"We will work on it," Noelle said.

Lucy snorted. "Well, my gut tells me that floozy at the senior home just made it up to get her hooks into the death benefit. Okay, I'll do whatever you need me to do," Lucy volunteered. "See you in the morning," she told Noelle, kissing her forehead. And then she looked at Duncan. "What about you, will I see you in the morning?"

Taken aback at the casual question and its obvious implication, Noelle cried, "Lucy!"

"Well, I was just wondering," Lucy said innocently. Her eyes swept over her granddaughter and Duncan. "We're all adults here, no reason to be embarrassed."

"I can think of one," Noelle murmured, eyeing her grandmother pointedly.

Lucy sighed. "Do something with her," she told Duncan, patting him on the arm as she passed him. "And keep me posted about Henry," she said over her shoulder as she walked out.

Feeling exceedingly antsy and somewhat nervous, Noelle crossed to the kitchen and opened the refrigerator. "Want some dinner?" she asked.

Duncan followed her into the small kitchen. "As long as I'm not putting you out," he said. "I guess I could eat."

She turned to look at him. He sounded rather vague about that. "You're not hungry?"

"I filled up on nuts at the bar," he told her.

There'd been so much activity at Malone's, she hadn't noticed whether he was eating something or not. "What do you usually have?" she asked, searching the refrigerator again. Nothing there tempted her or really lent itself to whipping up a decent meal.

Duncan shrugged casually in response to her question. "Anything I can get at a drive-through."

"You don't cook?"

He grinned. "Does pressing buttons on the microwave count?"

"Not really. I guess that Andrew's talents didn't rub off on you," she speculated.

The appetite that was currently raising its head within him had nothing to do with food.

Duncan came around the small kitchen table to stand right next to her.

"Hey, until a year ago, I didn't even know there *was* an Andrew, much less that he was my uncle. Probably wouldn't have known, either, if Brennan hadn't been working undercover for the DEA."

She couldn't fathom what one had to do with the other. "You're not going to just leave that sentence dangling like that, are you?"

There was mischief in his eyes as he said, "I was thinking about it. Why?" he asked. "Would that drive you crazy?"

"Yes," she cried with no hesitation.

His eyes skimmed over her face. "Then I'd say we'd be even."

Why did she feel as if the kitchen had suddenly grown smaller? And hotter? Definitely hotter. "How would we be even?"

There was a tug-of-war going on inside of him. Either way, he was going to lose. "Because wondering something about you has been driving me crazy for the last six months," he admitted quietly.

"We've only been working for the last six months."

He never took his eyes off her lips. "Exactly."

"And what is it, *exactly,* that you've been wondering about for the last six months?" she asked.

The question was barely audible.

Chapter 13

Instead of answering her question right away, Duncan slipped his fingers into her hair, cupping the back of her head.

Bringing her closer to him.

His lips covered hers, making not just her breath stop, but time and space, as well.

For both of them.

"That," he answered, his voice low, intimate, husky when he finally drew away from her. "I've been wondering about that. About what it would be like to kiss you."

"And what's the final verdict?" Noelle heard herself asking.

"Not sure yet," Duncan murmured. His heart was

pounding, but he did his best to ignore it. "I need more input."

"Then by all means, input," Noelle urged, positioning herself directly in front of him. Her body fitting up against his, she wove her arms around his neck and tilted her head back, making her lips even more accessible to his.

He kissed her. Kissed her as if he hadn't just kissed her a moment ago. Kissed her as if the whole experience was completely new to him and he had discovered exactly what it was about life that made it worth living.

Gathering her to him as if she were the very lifeline to his existence, Duncan kissed her long and deep until he and Noelle were both out of breath, singularly and collectively.

When Duncan finally drew his lips away from hers and the insane beating of her heart had toned down to a simple roar rather than the deafening echo of thunder, Noelle gazed up at him, struggling to collect all the countless pieces she had suddenly disintegrated into, so that she could reconstruct herself, at least to some extent.

Part of her felt that she would never be the same again.

"So?" she whispered hoarsely, "What's your conclusion now?"

It took Duncan a few seconds to find his tongue and remember how to use it.

"That I shouldn't have waited six months."

He'd no sooner uttered the last word than his lips had found hers again. The wild whirlwind of a ride began all over again, sending her head spinning and arousing feelings and responses from within her that, after the last time, after Christopher had died and her heart had been crushed, she had tried so very hard to bury.

Buried or not, they were back, out in force and reminding her that whatever else she had become and was, she was still very much a woman with a woman's desires and needs.

Desires and needs that demanded to be addressed.

Kissing him like this was making her summarily crazy. She didn't know how much longer she could hold herself in check.

For the second time that evening, Duncan drew his head away. "I'll stop if you want me to."

She stared at him in stunned disbelief. "Just like that?"

"No, I'll probably implode," he allowed. "But as far as continuing along this path, if you don't want to—"

"Oh, God, I want to," she assured him before he could finish his sentence. Grabbing on to his shirt, Noelle anchored him in place. And then she took a deep breath as a tiny measure of sanity made its way back to her. "But not here." Before he could ask her what she meant, Noelle took his face between her hands to get his undivided attention. "Upstairs. My bedroom."

Location—even a mattress—made no difference. He would have been willing to let what was happening between them sweep them both away right here.

And then it hit him.

They *had* to take this somewhere more private. What if her daughter suddenly wandered out of her room, maybe even drawn out by their revelry. He didn't want to be responsible for possibly creating nightmares for the little girl, for introducing her way too soon to something that, in its proper place and context, was lightning in a bottle, pure and simple.

The very best human experience possible.

But visually intercepted, it was also enough to scar a six-year-old for a very long time.

"Right," he agreed, physically and mentally putting himself on hold. "Lead the way. Show me where it is."

She took his hand as if they were both just teenagers and had him follow her up the stairs, bringing him to her room.

The second she closed the door, he spun her around to face him.

"I believe I left off *here*," he said, emphasizing the word as his mouth covered hers again.

She raised herself up on her toes, falling into the ever-growing fiery pit he had created for her. The flames felt as if they were all around her, licking at her body, heating it to unbelievably high levels. Desire fairly crackled within her.

Noelle pressed her body against his, seeking out his heat, searching for gratification.

Never in his wildest dreams would he have predicted that there was such a hellcat living just beneath his partner's straitlaced exterior. Having Noelle kiss him back just as eagerly as he kissed her, he was surprised to discover that they were almost on an equal footing when it came to this explosive game of tease and possess.

Clothes were shed and tossed aside as the strong motivation to get closer overtook them.

It was a game, a game he'd played countless times before, Duncan kept reminding himself.

Except that somewhere along the line, between just absorbing the heat of her body and discovering the marvels and joys of their two naked bodies intertwining with one another, he realized that it had ceased being so much a game as it became something else.

Something a great deal more.

What the definition of that was, he found he was almost powerless to say. An adequate description eluded him at this particular point.

All he knew was that the memory of countless women who had come before faded from his mind. And gradually, by evening's end, those memories had been completely erased.

Moreover, there was no satiating point, nothing that had him finally gasping and settling back into a contented sleep.

This time, this multifaceted hellcat he was with had aroused such a hunger within him, it made Duncan feel as if there was no point where he could stop. No point where the overwhelming craving would stop.

He just wanted this moment to continue.

He found himself just wanting to bring Noelle up and over these heights he seemed to be able to create for her, causing climaxes to flower into one another, claiming her over and over again and in so doing, bringing her enormous pleasure.

It made him feel eighteen feet tall, both powerful and humbled at the very same time.

He could feel the way those climaxes built and dovetailed for her by the way Noelle dug her fingertips into his shoulders, struggling to muffle cries of sheer ecstasy.

She made him weak.

She made him feel humble that it could be this way between a man and a woman. In that one instance, as he realized that his final moment—his complete release—was about to overtake him, Duncan suddenly thought he could empathize with what had gone through Brennan's head when his brother had committed to the woman he'd wound up marrying, turning his back on the playground he had always frequented. The one that he'd been more than welcomed to frequent for many years to come.

Immersing himself in the many did not compare to becoming part of the one.

The very thought, coming from nowhere, stunned Duncan.

Gathering Noelle so that she was totally beneath him, Duncan shifted his weight until he was over her.

Then, his heart once again pounding and his mouth sealed to hers, he entered her, melding, becoming one in every way.

An emotion flowed through him. For now, he tried to block it.

The sound of her increased rate of breathing excited him.

And then he felt her begin to move, inducing him to join in the rhythm, to mimic the movement, and soon they were clinging to one another for dear life, stopping time and sealing themselves in eternity for as long as they were allowed.

Stardust, she could have sworn that bursts of stardust had fallen all around her when that final glorious moment of free-falling ecstasy had surrounded him. Making him feel as close to immortal as was possible for someone to feel.

And then, all too soon, it was over and the earth rose up to meet them.

"Now what?" she asked, catching herself clinging to Duncan, trying to hold on to a split second of happiness for just a little longer.

It slipped through her fingers anyway.

Noelle blew out a long breath and then drew an equally long one in. It took a while for the pulses in her body to return to almost normal. But they did.

Finally.

Turning her head toward Duncan, she asked, "Now what?"

"I could applaud," he told her with the straightest face she had ever seen on him. "Because that's what you do when your mind's been blown."

"Idiot," she laughed.

"Or, I could lie here and let you insult me to your heart's content if you'd rather do that," he said. "I'm flexible."

God, there was an understatement, she thought. Her mouth curved as she responded to his last "suggestion" and she murmured, "My heart doesn't want to insult you."

He tucked her a wee bit closer against him. "Good to know."

They might as well face this and get it out of the way. Otherwise, it was going to only grow larger and larger, an obstacle for them to come to grips with down the line. Now was better. "But we did just cross a line here."

"Line?" he repeated with studied innocence. "I didn't see any lines," he said. "Stars, yes. Lines, no."

Doubling her fists, she punched his shoulder. "You know what I mean."

"O'Banyon, right now I don't even know what *I* mean," he confessed. Raising himself up on his elbow, he looked at her, an earnest expression on his face for a fleeting moment. "You changed the rules on me."

Was he being serious, or just teasing her? She couldn't tell. "What does that mean?" Noelle asked.

The sigh was a soulful one—and one of surrender. "It means I want to make love with you again."

Wasn't that what the past hour had been about? "Now?" she cried.

"Now," Duncan repeated. His expression was playful, but his tone was deadly serious as he added, "Next week, next month. Three days after Tuesday."

She put her fingers to his lips to stop him as she said, "I'm confused."

"*You're* confused?" Duncan laughed shortly, shaking his head. "Lady, I wouldn't recommend visiting my head right now." And then he lay down again, turning his body in toward hers. "Speaking of right now…"

She could feel his body hardening, wanting her. The excitement within her was growing at an almost frightening rate. "Yes?"

"I figure we shouldn't let all this nakedness just go to waste," he theorized, the light in his eyes teasing her. "It just doesn't seem right."

The feelings inside of her worried Noelle.

She knew exactly what was happening—what she had *sworn* she would never allow to happen again—and it scared her. Badly. But she just couldn't make herself get up and walk away from it.

From him.

"So what do you propose we do?"

"Give me some time to think on it," Duncan said as he began to skim his fingers along her breasts. "It'll come to me."

It was happening again, the longing was seizing her in a viselike grip. Making her want him with a fierceness she couldn't subdue. "How much time?"

"Not much," Duncan promised. His mouth curved as she turned into his caresses. "I am a fast study."

She was about to comment on that, but found she couldn't.

His lips had already found hers again and that insanely wild ride on the speeding roller coaster was beginning all over again.

What was most surprising to her was that her desires had all returned in full force, not a single one was remotely worn or diminished in the slightest way by having had made love with him just a few short minutes ago.

The passions, the needs, they had all reappeared in powerful force, each bringing her up to heights that were dizzying, almost terrifying, but oh-so thrilling all the same.

As an edginess began to nibble away at her, Noelle made love with Duncan, knowing full well that when tomorrow actually did come, all this was going to seem like an impossible dream, never to be realized again.

This, she told herself, was going to have to last her until forever.

* * *

The persistent buzzing crawled its way into her subconscious, burrowing in between the layers. It grew louder and louder. Loud enough to register with her brain.

The buzzing slowly became identifiable. A cell phone.

Was that her cell phone, trapped beneath the layers of her hastily thrown off clothing, vibrating and trying to get her attention?

The sudden thought had her bolting upright just in time to see Duncan getting up to look for his own cell phone.

"Talk about a rude awakening," Duncan muttered. He heard her suck in her breath behind him. He had hoped to find out who was calling before it woke her up. Turning around, he saw her watching him somewhat uncertainly.

Was she having regrets? Duncan wondered. "What's wrong?"

God, but she really was a magnificent sight, he couldn't help thinking. Earlier, desire had colored his perception. But that wasn't the case now and she was still as bone-meltingly gorgeous as she had been when they had first begun making love.

"You're naked," she said.

"I didn't think I needed to get dressed to look for my cell. I think yours is ringing, too. Your cell phone," he added in case she'd lost the thread of the conversation. She was holding her sheet against her. He found the display of modesty almost sweet.

Sweet?

What the hell was going on with him? he silently demanded.

And why, after that exhaustive go-round, did he find himself reacting to the way she was looking at him?

"Can't find your phone?" Noelle asked shyly. She knew she shouldn't be staring at him like this, but Duncan appeared to be so completely comfortable in his body that she found that she was having trouble making herself look away.

"I lost it somewhere," he said, smiling. He forced himself to get back to searching through the scattered clothing. Duncan moved a few more articles around—instead of ignoring the ringing and climbing back into bed with her.

"Ah, found it," he announced, plucking his cell phone from beneath the heap just beneath one of the two windows in the room. Opening the phone, he put it to his ear and announced, "Cavanaugh."

Noelle saw him listening, saw the serious look on his face and her attention was undividedly his as she tried to gauge what he could possibly be hearing on the other end. Was that a girlfriend calling him at this hour?

And why was that the first thing that popped into her head?

The man had millions of relatives, maybe one

of them was calling about something, some family business. Wouldn't that be more likely than his being tracked down in the middle of the night by some girlfriend or other?

Get a grip, Noely, she ordered herself. *He's your partner, not your boyfriend.*

It didn't help.

"Right away," Duncan was saying, and then he terminated the call.

"You have to leave?" she guessed the moment he put down the cell.

"*We* have to leave," Duncan amended her question. "Unless you'd rather that I handled this alone." As he talked, he gathered together his clothing, separating them from hers.

She forgot to hold the sheet against her as she leaned forward and asked, "Handle what alone?"

He glanced in her direction, meaning only to answer her question. However, seeing her like that caused him to take a minute to remember what he was going to say. "Some homeless guy was just the victim of a hit-and-run."

She waited for more, but he'd paused. "And this concerns us how?" she asked.

"I asked Bridget—one of my cousins," he explained even though Noelle hadn't asked who that was, "to pass the word around in Homicide that we needed them to keep an eye out for certain details in the murders that came across their desks."

"What kind of details?" she asked.

"That homeless guy—he's dead by the way," he informed her, "turns out that he had a life insurance policy in the pocket of his oversize coat. The policy was written out for *him*."

Noelle was out of bed in a flash, grabbing her cell from the floor. She didn't even bother to sit down again before hitting the very first button on speed dial.

Wearing just his jeans, Duncan came around to her side of the bed. "Who are you calling?" he asked.

"Lucy," she told him as she heard the phone on the other end ringing. "She's going to have to stay with Melinda."

"Shouldn't you get dressed before calling?" he asked her. Although he had to admit that he liked the view from here just the way it was.

She merely shook her head. "I can be dressed in five minutes," she promised.

No woman could get dressed in five minutes, he thought. Looking around for his own shirt, he found it and quickly pulled it on over his head.

"Five minutes? This I have to see." He made it sound almost like a dare.

"Six minutes if you watch," she amended.

Duncan grinned at her. The idea of watching her get dressed was only slightly less appealing than watching her get *un*dressed.

"Make it ten and I'll share my popcorn with you," he promised.

Noelle arched one reproving eyebrow as she regarded him. "You don't have any popcorn," she pointed out.

Duncan shrugged. "Minor detail."

He fell backward onto the bed when she pushed him. At the last moment, Duncan grabbed her hand and took her down with him.

Getting dressed had to wait.

Chapter 14

Lucy arrived less than twenty minutes after receiving her granddaughter's call. She didn't look surprised to see that Duncan was still on the premises. On the contrary, she gave him—as well as the situation—a quick, approving nod as she sailed past the detective at the front door. "I see you decided to stick around, Duncan."

Noelle could just hear Lucy going on about this the next time they were alone. Her only hope was if the woman bought her denial. At any rate, it was worth a shot.

"Actually, Cavanaugh just came by to pick me up," Noelle told her, hurrying down the stairs. She tried to discreetly adjust the clothing she had hastily thrown on after she and Duncan had undertaken one more, albeit extremely quick, go-round for the road.

"Really?" Lucy asked. The woman slanted another, more scrutinizing look in Duncan's direction. "They don't pay you detectives much, do they?"

"What makes you say that?" Duncan asked.

"Well, your clothing allowance has to be pretty meager." Lucy's eyes swept over him. "You're wearing the same clothes you had on when you dropped her off here earlier," the woman observed. "Not that you don't look good in them," she quickly followed up.

"Melinda's still asleep," Noelle interjected, hoping to divert her grandmother's attention. The last thing she needed was to have Lucy scrutinizing details. "You can stretch out in my room if you like." She'd made sure to remake the bed, taking extra care to leave no signs of Duncan's presence or the lovemaking they'd shared.

"You're not planning on coming back tonight?" Lucy asked, looking at Duncan significantly.

"Never know how these things can go," Duncan told her.

"If I get back before morning, I can always sleep on the couch," Noelle assured her. Pausing to kiss her grandmother's cheek, she added, "Thanks for coming to the rescue."

"Anytime," Lucy replied. "Stay safe!" she called after her granddaughter and Duncan as they left the house.

"She didn't buy it, you know," Duncan told her as they made their way down the driveway to the curb where his sedan was parked. "Lucy's a sharp little lady. She wasn't buying that bit about my coming by to pick you up." Especially since his vehicle was parked in exactly the same place it had been when Lucy had left for home hours earlier.

With a sigh, Noelle stood back, waiting for him to unlock his car. "I know."

"Then why bother saying it?" he asked. Unlocking her side first, he held the door open for her. A first in their case, he realized. Apparently the past few hours had left their impression.

Noelle got in and began wrestling with an uncooperative seat belt. "Because you don't just tell your grandmother that you're making love with a guy who's your partner at work."

Satisfied that she'd buckled up, Duncan started up his car. "She's a pretty cool lady." Glancing in his rearview mirror, he pulled away from the curb and wove his way out of her development. They were the only moving vehicle out at this hour. "I don't think that would have shocked her."

The word made Noelle laugh. "Lucy doesn't get shocked, she's usually the one doing the shocking," she said. When he slanted a glance in her direction, she responded with a vague shrug. "She has some very definite strong appetites, that's all I'm going to say on the subject."

His imagination took it from there and he grinned

broadly. "No wonder Shamus looked like he'd died and gone to heaven at Brennan and Tiana's wedding. Lucy probably tickled him down to his very toes. Family talk has it that he's thinking of asking her out."

As much as she wanted her grandmother to find someone to care about outside of just her and Melinda, the thought of Lucy getting involved with a Cavanaugh might not be such a good idea. "Listen, if you care about him, maybe you should talk him out of that."

He hadn't expected that kind of a reaction from Noelle. "Why?"

There was no other way to say it but to say it. "Lucy's fickle."

It was her turn to wonder when her response made him laugh.

"Number one," Duncan enumerated, "Shamus is *not* going to listen to anything a new relative has to tell him—he's a stubborn old man—and number two, it's not like he's looking for a long-term relationship to last the next half century. Hell, the man's close to eighty. I think he's earned the right to just say 'live and let live.' If Lucy makes him happy, let the man enjoy himself."

Noelle was silent for a second. She supposed that Duncan was right. She'd be the first to admit that she had a tendency to worry too much. "I guess that's not such bad advice."

His eyes met hers for a second. "Depends on who it's for," he replied vaguely.

Noelle couldn't have explained why, but she had the strangest feeling that Duncan was putting her on some sort of notice.

No, he's not. Get a grip, Noely.

It was just her imagination, she silently insisted. She had allowed her guard to slip and now she was supervulnerable. Vulnerable to actions and to suggestions, as well. Coupled with her overactive imagination and she could very easily drive herself crazy, Noelle silently warned herself. As wonderful as the past few hours had been, she should *not* have allowed them to happen.

Yeah, right, the same little voice in her head mocked.

She struggled to rein her imagination and her emotions back to their original borders, the ones that had been in place yesterday morning.

Sparing a look at Duncan's chiseled, sexy profile, she realized she was going to have a *real* struggle on her hands.

She needed to get back to work, to dive headfirst into details. It was the only way she was going to survive.

Blowing out a breath, she sat back in her seat. "So what do we know about this homeless guy?"

Duncan reiterated the first piece of information he'd gotten. "He was a hit-and-run victim a couple of days ago."

"A couple of days ago?" she echoed. Why the time lag? The case either fell into their purview or it didn't. That should have been evident immediately, shouldn't it? "And we're just hearing about it now?"

"No one thought to call Vice over a hit-and-run," he said, emphasizing the name of their department. "But after I told Bridget to keep her ears open for anything that might be part of the case we're working on, she recalled someone talking about the homeless guy having an insurance policy premium notice in his pocket. She thought we'd want to follow up on that."

Duncan took the left turn quickly, barely making it through the yellow light before it turned red. Noelle braced her hand against the dashboard to keep from leaning into him. It was on the tip of her tongue to ask him why his cousin had chosen to call him about it at *this* hour, but she decided that this Bridget was probably on the night shift and had most likely just found out about the hit-and-run.

"Another strange thing according to Bridget," Duncan continued, "was that for a homeless guy, he was pretty clean. He didn't smell, his hair was washed and he'd had a shave."

"So maybe he wasn't homeless," she speculated. "Why would Bridget think he was?"

That, at least, had a simple answer. "Because when he was found, the uniforms canvassing the area talked to a few of the homeless guys camped out under the 5 overpass and they said he was one of them. One of the homeless guys referred to him as Alfie."

This was getting really involved and confusing, Noelle thought. Closing her eyes, she leaned back against her headrest and murmured softly to herself, "What's it all about, Alfie?"

The classic tagline from an old movie rang a bell for Duncan. "You're familiar with that?" he asked, surprised.

She opened her eyes again and sat up a little straighter. "With what?"

"Alfie," he repeated. "You just quoted a line from the movie as well as from the theme song. It was a classic." Opening himself up a little more to her, he added, "They remade the movie a while back."

"Let me guess, you're an old movie buff." Now, there was something she would have never guessed.

"Not obsessively," he replied, then admitted, "but I have seen my fair share of old movies." He could see that she appeared to be amused by the thought of him watching movies over half a century old. "Hey, when you're on stakeout night after night, you need something to while away the time."

His admission made him a little more human in her eyes—not that she was about to say so. She felt she'd already gotten in way too deep as it was.

"I get it. You don't have to explain yourself to me," she said.

Changing the subject, Duncan gave voice to the

question that was on both their minds. "What's a homeless guy doing with a life insurance policy?"

She raised her shoulders in a hopeless, confused movement. "Beats me. Maybe he got lucky, found work and started to turn his life around."

"I can buy into that, but why get a life insurance policy?" he pressed. "People get policies to provide for someone else if they're suddenly not around."

"Maybe this guy *had* a someone else," she said, thinking out loud.

"First stop is the morgue," he decided, making a right turn at the next corner. "We're going to need a picture of this guy to show around to those homeless people the uniforms talked to."

Only one problem with that. "*If* they're still there," Noelle qualified.

"Let's hope so," he said, stepping on the gas.

Edwin Addams dropped his apple when he looked up. The sound of the door to the morgue opening had caught his attention. He jumped up from the stool he'd been perched on.

"What did I do?" he demanded, glaring at Noelle. "Tell me what did I do. Who did I tick off?"

Noelle crossed to the coroner. Duncan was right beside her. "What makes you think you ticked someone off—although you probably did," she allowed.

The scowl only grew deeper. "Because you keep turning up here to pester me."

Stooping down to pick up his apple, she offered it

to him. When he completely ignored it, she put the apple on the stool. "Just lucky, I guess," she told the man. "Don't worry, Addams, we're not staying. We just need to take a picture."

"What kind of a picture?" he asked suspiciously.

"The kind you snap with a cell phone," Duncan answered for her.

Looking like a man whose head was about to explode, the coroner drew in a deep breath and tried again. "Of who?"

"You picked up a hit-and-run victim two days ago," she said. "A guy named Alfie. Has anyone come by to claim him?"

The heavyset man lumbered over to the large board he had on the opposite wall. He squinted at it for a moment. "It says his niece is sending someone to pick up his body in the morning, so I guess you're in luck. He's still with us." Sarcasm dripped from every syllable.

"His niece?" Noelle repeated, exchanging a puzzled glance with her partner. "We were under the impression that he had no family."

"I guess you can just crawl out from under that impression because it says here that he does." Addams jabbed a pudgy finger at the line where the homeless victim's information was written. "Now, are we done here?" Addams demanded.

Noelle took out her cell phone and held it up for the man. "We need a picture, remember?"

Rather than answer directly, he waved for them

to follow him. "C'mon." The coroner's tone was less than inviting.

Reaching the opposite end of the room, Addams was breathing heavily, as if he had taken part in some sort of a marathon rather than just crossing the room.

"That one," he said, pointing to the second drawer from the top, third row from the left.

Duncan opened it and then pulled out the body residing inside on the slab. The man's grayish face was a mass of cuts, contusions and bruises.

"Wow," Noelle commented under her breath, shaken by the sight.

Addams looked at her, his disapproval glaringly apparent. "It was a hit-and-run, what did you expect?" the coroner asked.

"Not quite so much damage," Noelle admitted. "He looks like he was not only hit, but dragged." Bracing herself, she snapped two shots in quick succession, verifying that each had come out looking as decent as possible under the circumstances.

Pocketing the cell phone, she turned toward the coroner and murmured, "Thanks," then said the words she knew he was dying to hear, "we'll get out of your hair now."

"Don't rush out on my account," Addams retorted sarcastically.

"We could stay awhile," Duncan deadpanned, turning to face Addams.

A look of horror instantly came over the coroner's

face. The next second, he ordered them to leave in less-than-dulcet tones. "Get out."

"You really do need to work on your social skills," Noelle told the man as she walked out of the room. "Someone might get the idea that you don't like them. Not me, of course." She deliberately grinned at him as she left.

"I think the man must live at the morgue," she said to Duncan as they walked down the long, dimly lit corridor.

"Given the hour and the fact that we found Addams there, you're probably right." Reaching the one lone elevator, he pressed the up button. "Are you buying this niece story?"

The elevator doors opened almost before he removed his finger from the button and they got on. Noelle jabbed at the button that would take them to the first floor. "Well, stranger things have happened and he was cleaned up, despite the marks he had from the accident. Shave, hair cut. Could be he reconnected with a long-estranged family member. Those clothes he had on looked as if they were relatively new. Maybe he did come into some luck. Too bad it didn't last."

"Or maybe," Duncan speculated as they got off, "that luck he came into was only supposed to last for a limited time."

Noelle watched him with interest. Right now, she was open to any theory. They needed something to tie all this together if they were going to make a case—and in her bones, she had a feeling that these deaths *were* connected.

"Go on," she urged.

"Whoever got him cleaned up—this mysterious niece or maybe someone else—might have had an ulterior motive in mind," he pointed out.

They had one thing staring them in the face. "Like collecting on the life insurance?"

His mouth curved as he nodded. She was having trouble keeping her mind on the subject at hand. His smile had instantly brought back memories of their night together.

She needed to put a lid on that, she silently lectured herself.

"That's what I'm thinking," Duncan was saying. He went back to something he'd suggested while they were driving to the morgue. "Why don't we go back to the overpass and see if any of this guy's buddies are still there and in the mood to talk."

"Absolutely," she agreed. "But let's stop at a fast-food place first."

He looked at her in surprise. "You're hungry?" he asked.

"Not particularly, but they probably are," she told him as they headed back to his sedan. "Nothing loosens a tongue like a full belly."

"You're more devious than I thought. This is definitely going down in the books as a night of revelations about you, O'Banyon," he said.

What else, she couldn't help wondering, was he putting down in that "book"?

A homeless man who seemed far too overdressed for the weather and rocked slightly to and fro as they spoke to him was the first to be lured out from the cardboard shelter where he was sleeping. He stared now at the photo image on the cell phone being held up in front of him. Dirty, trembling fingers held tightly onto the half-finished double cheeseburger he'd been given.

"Yeah, that's Alfie. That's him." He shook his head, looking genuinely upset. "Man, just when he thought he had a shot at getting back on his feet, that happens. There's no justice. No justice," he lamented, taking another large bite of the burger. One last bite and the burger was history.

"What kind of a shot?" Noelle asked, slipping another burger into his hand, trading it for the empty wrapper he held.

Looking grateful, the man paused to take another large bite. This time he chewed before swallowing. "That lady who came by a couple of months ago, he told me she had a job for him, that if things went well, he'd be earning good money for his trouble." Noelle thought she'd never seen such sadness when he told them, "Alfie said he'd come back for me. Guess he won't, now."

"Did he happen to say her name?" Duncan pressed.

"Was it Susan?" Noelle asked, remembering the name of the woman who Johnson had said befriended his neighbor.

"No, it wasn't Susan." Hapless shoulders rose and fell. "It was some state name," the man said. He looked as if he was literally straining his brain, trying to remember. "Georgia—no, that wasn't it."

"Virginia?" Noelle asked. It was the only other state that came to mind.

The dirty face seemed to almost light up with recognition. "Yeah, that was it, Virginia. Her name was Virginia. Pretty."

"Would you happen to know what kind of a job she was offering Alfie?" Duncan asked.

The homeless man shook his head. "He never said. Just that it was easy."

Noelle scrolled through the pictures on her phone until she came to the sketch that had been drawn after Johnson had described the woman who had gotten his neighbor to buy a life insurance policy.

"Did she look anything like this?" she asked, showing the homeless man the drawing.

He squinted, staring, then took another bite before answering. "Maybe. I'm not sure. She was pretty," he told them again. "But not young like you," he added, watching her. "I think Alfie had a thing for her."

They were finally getting somewhere, Noelle thought, eagerly pressing for more. "Do you remember anything else? Was she tall, short, thin, fat—"

"Tall, thin. She had blond hair, maybe light

brown. I'm not sure," he admitted. As he thought, he finished the second burger. "I was kinda out of it that night she came by. It was the anniversary of the day my wife ran out on me and I kinda wanted to dull the pain. Had a little too much to drink, I guess. Sorry," he apologized, looking genuinely repentant in her opinion.

"Don't be sorry," Noelle told him. "You've been a great help." She pressed a twenty into the man's filthy hand. "That's for more food," she said. "Not for *pain duller,* understand?"

The man bobbed his head up and down so hard, she thought for a moment that he might make himself dizzy. "Yes, ma'am."

"Okay," Noelle said, turning back to her partner. "Let's see if anyone else can remember seeing Alfie's benefactress."

"She was either that or one hell of a lethal con artist," Duncan countered.

"My money's on con artist," Noelle said.

She and Duncan went back to the overpass to see if they could get any further details about this woman.

Chapter 15

Two hours of questioning the handful of homeless people staking out a tiny bit of space beneath the overpass yielded no further information for them to go on. None of the three men and one woman admitted even to seeing the woman who had singled Alfie out, apparently taking him under her wing and away from the impromptu encampment.

"I don't get it," Noelle complained as they walked back to the white sedan. "How can—I'm assuming—a fairly well-dressed woman supposedly make her way around a homeless encampment without anyone seeing her?" she shook her head, frustrated.

Duncan glanced over his shoulder at the people they'd just talked to. "Because all they want to do is to disappear. A lot of these people are either rabidly in denial of their situation, or so deep into finding ways to numb themselves to the pain of what they've gone through, *are* going through, that they shut out everything around them. It's a mind-set. We're lucky to have found that one guy to talk to us," he said, referring to the first homeless man they had encountered.

"You sound as if you have firsthand information about that kind of life—or lack thereof."

"Secondhand," he corrected.

That still didn't answer her question. "Care to elaborate?"

"Brennan."

"Elaborate a little more," she coaxed, banking down a wave of impatience.

Now that his brother's career had moved on, Duncan felt he was free to talk about it. "Brennan spent a lot of time undercover, part of that was as a homeless man, sleeping in doorways, hunting for food in Dumpsters behind restaurants. The stories he told would have sent shivers down your spine. They did for me," he readily admitted.

"I'll take your word for it," she said to Duncan. Her phone began to buzz, emitting a strange rhythmic noise. Rather than look surprised to be on the receiving end of a call so early in the morning, Noelle dug her cell out of her pocket and shut it off without bothering to glance at the small screen.

"You're not taking the call?" he asked.

"That's not a call, that's my alarm," she said. They'd spent more time out here than she'd thought. "I'm sorry, but I've got to make a quick stop at the house."

"No problem," he told her. "I was planning on bringing you back to your place so you could pick up your car. This way you won't feel as if you have to wait for me if you want to check something out on your own." Why did she have an alarm set for seven-thirty in the morning? he wondered. "Anything wrong?"

"No," she answered, then added, "Thanks for asking. I just like making contact with Melinda in the morning before she goes to school if I can." They'd reached his vehicle, but she didn't get in. "Gives her a sense of continuity."

Duncan read between the lines. "The kind you didn't have."

The ship that protected that particular piece of her private life had already set sail, she thought, so there was no point in her denying his assumption.

"Not until I went to live with Lucy," she acknowledged. "Look, if you want to go directly to the precinct, I can call for a cab."

Cop or not, this was not the kind of place he felt she should be left by herself, waiting around for a cab to arrive.

"I said I'd take you. Look, in case you missed this in Police Basics 101, I'm your partner. That means I have your back. In everything," Duncan emphasized, then went on to offer, "I can have it stitched on a T-shirt if it'll help you remember."

"You're my partner, we have each other's backs, yes, I got that," she informed him, then hesitated for a moment before continuing. "It's just that, well, after last night, I thought maybe you'd rather not have to spend that much time with me, at least for a while."

He stared at her over the hood of his car. "You didn't happen to accidentally hit your head during all that energized activity last night, did you?" he asked.

He actually looked serious when he put the question to her, so she answered, "No—"

"Then where in the name of everything that makes sense did you get a dumb idea like that?" he demanded.

She didn't know whether to take offense at his tone, or rejoice at the meaning behind the question. She waffled somewhere in between. "I just didn't want you to feel that I was being clingy."

Duncan got into his car and put his seat belt on, then waited for her to do the same before he put his question to her.

"Are you?"

Her eyes met his and she answered him with as much sincerity as she could. "No."

He put his key into the ignition and started up the engine. "Then we're fine—as long as you stop saying stupid things."

Noelle pressed her lips together, looking straight ahead rather than at him. "I'll work on it."

Duncan smiled to himself. His immediate future promised to be interesting, he couldn't help thinking. "See that you do."

"You're just in time to kiss her goodbye," Lucy announced when Noelle hurried into the house. There was an almost undetectable note of relief in the older woman's voice. "We're going to be late for school."

Melinda happily leaned into her mother as Noelle embraced her and kissed the top of her head.

"I told Lucy we couldn't go until you came to kiss me goodbye," Melinda told her mother. Then, turning toward Duncan, she included him in this family ritual by saying, "Momma always kisses me goodbye before I go to school."

Duncan nodded at the information. "So your mom was telling me. A goodbye kiss is very important," he agreed. "Guaranteed to start your day off right," he added with a degree of solemnity that instantly registered with the little girl.

Her eyes dancing, Melinda looked at her mother. "I like him, Mama. He's funny."

Holding Melinda to her one extra second, Noelle nodded. "I said the same thing myself."

"What, that you like me?" Duncan asked, his face devoid of expression and giving nothing away.

She was not about to admit anything, especially not in front of her grandmother and her daughter. "No, that you're funny. Okay, Babycakes, go with

Lucy and don't forget to learn something today," she called after the little girl.

"I will, Momma," Melinda promised with a happy squeal.

Lucy was not quite so gleeful. "Are you getting anywhere on the case?" she asked as she ushered her great-granddaughter out.

Noelle was not about to lie to the woman who'd raised her. Lucy deserved better than that. So she shook her head in response. "Maybe Henry's autopsy will tell us something."

Ever optimistic in the face of adversity, Lucy held her crossed fingers high above her head as she left with Melinda.

Later that morning, Henry's exhumation papers had been signed and filed with the proper authorities and the exhumation was being carried out even now. In addition, Noelle was aware that Duncan had gotten his uncle Sean to bump up the actual autopsy. The preliminary paper would be forthcoming some time today, although she knew that the tox screen would require more time.

But some information was better than none, Noelle reasoned.

Duncan picked up the thread that had been begun by his partner and Lucy. "Let's see if the M.E. has something yet."

"I think we need to check in to the squad room first so the lieutenant knows that there's been another body to add to the ever-expanding case," Noelle suggested, referring to Alfie, the homeless hit-and-run victim that Duncan's cousin had alerted him to.

Duncan nodded. "Jamieson probably already knows, but it wouldn't hurt to check in, just in case," he agreed.

But the second they walked into the lieutenant's small office, Jamieson informed them, "The chief of d's wants to see you two."

It was beginning to feel as if they were playing some sort of game of virtual tag, Duncan thought. "About the case?" he asked.

"That would be my guess," Jamieson responded. "By the way, anything new?" he asked as the two began to vacate his office.

"Just that there's been another victim," Duncan answered.

"Homeless guy?" Jamieson asked.

"Yes," Noelle answered. The speed with which news traveled was unbelievable, not to mention over-whelming.

"Already heard," Jamieson was looking back at the files that were spread out of his desk like so many sprawling pages.

"So much for catching Jamieson off guard," No-elle commented. Stepping into the elevator, she looked at Duncan. "What do you think your uncle wants to talk to us about?" she asked.

"The case," Duncan answered.

She suppressed a surge of annoyance. Of course it was going to be about the case. The chief of d's didn't socialize during work hours. "I meant specifically," she said.

Duncan shoved his hands into his pockets and shook his head. "Haven't a clue."

She found that somewhat hard to believe. "But he's your uncle."

"Not while we're on the job," Duncan pointed out. "Then he's the chief of detectives and our boss." And while he might not have liked that, Duncan added silently, he could respect it.

Noelle frowned as they got off the elevator again. "If that's supposed to make me feel better, it's not working."

Was she afraid of getting chewed out because they hadn't made the kind of progress that TV procedural episodes are made of? "He's got a reputation for being reasonable, that's all I can say."

"Hope you're right," she told her partner just before they entered Brian's outer office.

The tall, lanky administrative assistant told them that the chief was waiting for them. Noelle crossed her fingers behind her back just before she walked into Brian's office.

Brian glanced up from his work and then rose from his desk when he saw them. Crossing to the door, he closed it behind Noelle.

"Sit, please," he instructed, then came back around his own desk and did the same. Moving his chair in closer, he steepled his fingers before him and looked at the two detectives in front of his desk. The pause seemed inordinately long before he said, "I was told you had a body exhumed."

"We had permission," Noelle quickly volunteered.

Brian dropped his hands to his desk and folded them. The look on his face was patient and kind.

"Never crossed my mind that you didn't," he replied. "I was also told that you were the one who first made a connection between a number of senior citizens dying within six to eighteen months after they took out life insurance policies."

Noelle sat up a little straighter, feeling somewhat nervous as well as energized. "I thought it was kind of unusual," she admitted, still not knowing whether she was going to be commended or read the riot act for overstepping her authority.

Brian nodded as if conferring with some inner voice. "Nice catch. I like my detectives to be on their toes and not restricted by tunnel vision. I had Marvin put a rush on the autopsy," he told them, referring to Lewis Marvin, the medical examiner. "He promised to have the results on both our desks before noon today. If this turns out to become unwieldy and you need a task force, all you need to do is ask," he informed them, looking from Duncan to Noelle. His expression told them he was serious, that the words he'd just uttered were not without weight.

"Yes, sir. We'll keep that in mind," Noelle promised with enthusiasm.

Brian tried to remember if he had ever been this young and eager, even when he had been O'Banyon's age. He had a feeling the answer was no. But it was enthusiasm such as hers that brought cases to closure, that solved the grisly puzzles they were presented with every day.

He rose then, signaling that the interview was over and they were free to leave. "I'll like to be kept apprised of your progress and also if something else comes up," he told them.

"Yes, sir," Noelle responded without a second's hesitation.

"Of course, sir," Duncan replied with a little less enthusiasm than his partner was displaying. Turning, he followed Noelle out the door.

"Is it me, or does the chief of d's seem somehow bigger-looking in that office," Noelle asked her partner as soon as they were clear of the chief's assistant's desk.

"Not enough room for him and his shadow, I guess," Duncan speculated, then pointed out, "he is about six-four or so."

"He looked taller," Noelle said.

Duncan laughed. He knew exactly what she meant. He'd felt the same way the first time he'd stopped by the chief's office.

"He does have that effect on people," Duncan said.

They went back to the squad room and Duncan disappeared. When he returned, it was with a crime board that was mounted on wheels. He'd borrowed it from another department.

"I thought if we had everything up in front of us, maybe we could get to the bottom of this faster," he explained to Noelle as he parked the mobile board against the wall closest to them.

She liked the idea. "I'm willing to try anything."

Within half an hour, they had photographs of the four victims they were currently dealing with. Even as she tacked up the eight-by-ten pictures, Noelle had the uneasy feeling that there were probably more out there.

The other side of the coin was that she could be completely wrong about this, wrong that the deaths had been engineered for profit and were just horrible incidents.

"We're basing this all on a hunch, you know," Noelle told her partner quietly. "Right now, we don't even know if Sally and Henry were actually victims, or if this is all just some terrible coincidence and nothing more."

"Beginning to doubt yourself?" Duncan asked her. She couldn't read anything into his expression. Was he challenging her—or agreeing with her vacillation?

"No," she denied with feeling, then, because she wasn't 100 percent certain, she backtracked. "Maybe."

"You don't believe in coincidences, remember?"

he told her. And then Duncan sighed, dragging a hand through his unruly dark hair. "Maybe we're going about this the wrong way."

"What way would you like to go about this?" she asked.

"How about if we go at it from the life insurance policy angle?" Duncan suggested. "We find out what company or companies issued these policies, what agent or broker sold them, exactly how the monies were paid out and where the checks were sent. Not to mention just who's running these so-called charitable foundations that Lucy's friends named as their beneficiaries." These were all questions that he'd hoped Brenda would find the answers to; but since she'd gotten sick, they were still unanswered. That had to change.

Noelle blew out a breath. "Sounds like a really tall order."

"You have any better ideas?" he asked her.

Noelle shook her head. "Not a single one, better or not," she admitted.

"Okay, then for the time being," Duncan said, "let's start looking into these so-called life insurance policies that all these dead people were talked into getting."

"No offense, but offhand, I'd say that we need someone who's a lot more tech savvy than you or I are, and since Brenda's out, there's nobody in her department we can turn to. They're all swamped right now, trying to pick up her slack," Noelle pointed out.

"None taken," Duncan responded. "And you're right," he agreed with a sigh. And then he brightened as a solution occurred to him. "Valri."

"Who?" Oh, please God, don't let that be the name of another victim, she silently prayed.

"My sister Valri," Duncan told her. "You met her at the wedding. She's a uniform cop but I'm pretty sure we can temporarily get her reassigned to us and use her to track down the policies for us. Granted, she's not Brenda, but Valri's better than anyone else I know. With some more experience, she could turn into another Brenda."

"Valri," Noelle repeated. Duncan nodded. "Your sister." It wasn't a question but he nodded a second time anyway. She vaguely remembered being introduced but right now, she couldn't have picked Valri Cavanaugh out of a lineup. "Just how many sisters do you have, Cavanaugh?" she asked, feeling as if there were relatives coming out of the woodwork.

"Three," he replied. "And if you're counting, I've also got three brothers. Why do you ask?"

"No reason. Just feeling a little overwhelmed by the numbers, that's all."

"You're overwhelmed?" he laughed, leaning a hip against the side of his desk. "Try seeing it from my side. There always seemed to be a crowd whenever I looked around me."

At this point, she was still trying to get the names of his siblings—never mind about the cousins—straight. But the idea of there always being someone around when you felt like talking or sharing something deeply personal sounded wonderful to her. Growing up, as much as she loved Lucy, there were things she wanted to share with someone closer to her own age.

"You'll forgive me if I don't shed any tears over your plight," Noelle told him. "It must be a phenomenal feeling, having a support system like that any time you needed someone in your corner."

"Yeah, there was that," Duncan readily agreed. "But the flip side of that is that there was always someone that was being held up as an example—someone you weren't measuring up to."

"I didn't think of that," Noelle admitted—but she also doubted that it happened very often. Otherwise, Duncan wouldn't be as close to his siblings as she could see that he was.

Duncan shrugged, conceding the point to her since she didn't put up an argument. To be honest, he could understand why she seemed to envy him. His siblings could drive him crazy—but he couldn't think of anyone he would rather have in his corner.

"Like every situation," he mused, "this has its pluses and its minuses."

"Well, I'd put up with those minuses just to get a few of those pluses," she told him.

He grinned at her. "Yeah, just between you and me—me, too. Now if you'll excuse me, I have to go find out who I have to bribe in order to get Valri temporarily reassigned to us."

She glanced over her shoulder toward the lieutenant's office. "Maybe you'd better start with Jamieson, just to cover your bases. If he can help, problem's solved, if he can't, at least he'll know that you didn't go over his head without first consulting him—and then you can go back to the chief of d's. He did say to get back to him if we needed extra help."

Duncan nodded his approval of her suggestion. "You're learning, O'Banyon," he said as he headed toward the lieutenant's office. "You're learning."

She watched him as he walked away, thinking of their night together. "More than you'll ever know, Cavanaugh. More than you'll ever know," she whispered under her breath.

Chapter 16

"What's the catch?" Valri asked suspiciously. As blond as he was dark, Duncan's youngest sister narrowed her blue eyes to look more closely at him and the woman with him. Shorter than her brother by a good ten inches, she still had a sturdy, capable air about her despite the fact that she had never weighed more than 105 pounds in her life.

They were riding up the elevator to the squad room after he and Noelle had gone to her, saying that her sergeant had okayed her being temporarily loaned out to Vice.

"No catch," Duncan told her. "We've got something to track down in cyberspace and we thought you might be able to help us using that magic that you do with computers."

Valri had gotten a reputation as being the go-to person in the family when it came to anything computer-related, but that was strictly on a personal level.

The elevator reached their floor and the doors parted. "Isn't the chief's daughter-in-law in charge of that?" she asked as they got off.

"Officially, yes, but right now, she's out sick," Noelle answered.

"But she's got assistants," Valri pointed out.

"They're not as good as you are," Duncan said. "And right now they're swamped, trying to catch up since Brenda got sick."

Or, at least that was what he assumed. The truth of it was that he didn't have a working relationship with any of them. Getting Valri up here as part of their team meant that he could have her attention focused exclusively on unearthing the pieces of the puzzle they needed to help them find the person or persons responsible for four murders—and possibly more.

"Now you really have me worried," Valri said. "If the sergeant hadn't okayed this right in front of me, I'd swear that you were trying to mess with me and get me into some kind of trouble."

"How can you say that?" Duncan asked, putting his hands over his heart as if his sister's words had just fatally wounded him.

"Maybe because I know you so well," she countered.

"This is it, Valri," Noelle said, walking into the squad room ahead of Duncan's sister and gesturing around the area. "I can't tell you how much we really need your help."

Valri looked from her brother's partner to her brother. She caught Duncan's unguarded glance directed at Noelle. The next second it was gone, but she'd seen it nonetheless.

"Then again, maybe I don't know you as well as I think I do after all," Valri murmured under her breath.

Duncan had heard the sound of her voice but not the words. "What?"

"Nothing." Valri was quick to wave away her words. "Just trying to get comfortable with my surroundings."

"Good," Noelle said, "because the sooner you get comfortable, the sooner you'll be able to come up with as much information as you can find. Maybe it'll help piece together exactly what is going on for us."

They'd stopped before the bulletin board he had borrowed from another department to facilitate their hunt for the killer. "Why don't you fill my sister in on the background of the case?" he suggested to Noelle. Before she could ask him why he didn't want to do that himself, he added, "I was never much good at explaining things when it came to Valri."

"World's *worst* math tutor, bar none," Valri declared with feeling in what she pretended was a stage whisper.

Duncan had started to walk to his desk. "I heard that," he spoke up.

"You were supposed to," Valri informed him.

"Let's get started," Noelle said, ushering Duncan's sister over toward the front of the bulletin board and photographs of the first two victims.

They found an empty desk for Valri for the duration of her stay in Vice.

"As long as we wrap this case up in under two weeks," Duncan said loftily, "because that's when Anderson's coming back from his honeymoon." He placed a laptop in front of his sister that had initially been requisitioned by Brenda.

"No pressure, right?" Valri eyed the dormant computer "And who does the laptop belong to?" she asked.

"We managed to 'borrow' it from IT. One of Brenda's assistants said it's yours for as long as you need it," he informed his sister. "The assistant also sent his thanks."

"Why is he thanking me?" Valri asked.

Noelle fielded the question before her partner could. "Because this way, your brother's not down there, badgering them for their help. So anything you can do to keep their load from increasing, they probably view as a personal favor."

"Who knows, kid?" Duncan chimed in. "Play

your cards right and there might be a place for you downstairs in IT when the allure of patrolling the streets of this fair city starts to wane."

Valri frowned and turned her chair in Noelle's direction, facing away from her brother. "Does he talk like that all the time when he's up here?" she asked.

"Not really," Noelle confided, adding, "I think the performance is strictly for you."

Duncan looked from his partner to his sister. "You know, maybe this wasn't such a good idea, having you brought up here. I'm beginning to really feel outnumbered."

Coming around to his side, Noelle patted his face and smiled at him. "That's because you are, Cavanaugh."

"Well, I still outrank you," Duncan informed his sister. "And I have seniority over you," he said, turning toward Noelle.

Noelle held up a finger before he could retreat to his desk. "Yes, but the lieutenant made me lead on the case, remember?"

Valri slanted a glance at her brother and then looked back at his partner. A very pleased smile spread across her face. "Looks like you met your match, Duncan."

"Never mind that. You just get all the information you can on those policies for us," he instructed, pointing at the laptop.

"Yes, sir," Valri responded, executing a smart salute directed at her brother.

"Better," he said, nodding his approval at the display of obedience.

"You Detective O'Banyon?"

Noelle turned around to find a very young uniformed police officer standing behind her. He had the look of a lost puppy about him.

"Yes." That was when she saw the manila envelope in his hand. Noelle raised her eyes to the police officer's. "Is that for me?"

"Yes, ma'am, um, I mean, sir...I mean, um—" The police officer clearly appeared at a loss as to how to refer to her.

"*Detective* will do fine, Officer," she assured him, putting her hand out for the envelope.

For half a second, the young officer looked slightly bewildered. "Oh, right," he said belatedly as if remembering the nature of his errand. He placed the envelope in her hand. "The M.E. said you were in a hurry for this."

"That we are," she cried, excited. "Tell him we're all very grateful he was able to get this to us so quickly," she instructed as she pulled the pages out of the envelope.

Duncan had circled behind her in an instant, reading the report over her shoulder. "What's it say?" he asked her even as he began to read.

Noelle had already skimmed over enough of the report to find out what she wanted. "That Lucy was right," she told him. "Her friend should still be alive—the preliminary tox findings are that he was injected with a drug that made it look as if he'd had a heart attack," she said. "Just like Teasdale."

So it was murder. But that still didn't answer the most glaring question. "But why kill him?" Duncan asked.

"Logical answer is for the insurance money," Noelle said.

"Except that the money is supposedly going to some charitable foundation," he reminded her.

Her mind went into hyperdrive as she considered the different possibilities at that end. "Maybe the money is being diverted. Wouldn't be the first time that people were caught embezzling funds from some lofty charity or a trust fund. We really need to find out who runs the foundation," she said, looking over toward Valri.

"Foundations," Duncan corrected her. "Lucy said that she suspected it was likely both her friends were leaving money to different organizations."

"Maybe they're really the same foundation," she theorized. "We need to find out if Alfie and Walt left their death benefits to charitable foundations, as well." Turning around again to look at Duncan's sister, she said, "Valri—"

"Already on it," Valri assured her brother's partner, her fingers flying across the keyboard.

"She *is* good," Noelle said to her partner with no small appreciation.

Duncan inclined his head in silent agreement,

then cautioned, "I'd keep that to myself if I were you, she's already got a swelled head."

"I heard that," Valri piped up.

"You were supposed to," Duncan replied, echoing the words she had said to him just a few minutes ago.

"They were different," Valri spoke up sometime later. The sound of clicking keys had been nonstop as she'd conducted her hunt. Her tone was serious as she reported her findings thus far. "The organizations that the last two victims named in their life insurance polices were different from each other and different from the first two charitable organizations. Here are all four names. One supposedly is striving to find cures for something called 'orphan diseases,' another is dedicated to protecting an endangered species. There's one to promote bringing fresh water to impoverished countries in Africa and the last one claims its goal is to help bring about world peace." Valri paused for a moment as she scrolled back up on her screen. "What're orphan diseases? Is that something unique to orphans?"

Noelle remembered coming across an explanation of the designation in a magazine article she'd once read. "That's a term used for a disease that's so rare that there's no known funding to find a cure for it since so few people would benefit if one was discovered."

Valri looked back at the screen. "Well, that *sounds* like a worthy charity."

"I think that's the whole point," Duncan commented, coming around to take a look at what his sister had come up with. "Can you track down who runs that foundation and where it's located?"

Valri nodded, already inputting information to begin the search. She paused for a moment, reading. "Looks like there are several holding companies involved so this might take me a while to track down the various companies to a single source."

"Do what you can, kid," Duncan urged. "My money's on you."

As her brother began to walk back to his desk, Valri said, "I did find the name of one of the insurance companies that issued a policy."

Duncan pivoted on his heel, turning to face her again. "That's my girl," he declared. "What is it?"

"Woodland Life. They insured that old guy who ran into the pole. Walt," she recalled. "I'm still working on the others."

Maybe they could call the company and find out the name of the actual agent who sold the policy to Walt, Noelle thought. But not before she had some standard pieces of information.

She placed herself on Valri's right side. "We're going to need his date of birth and his social security number, as well as the face amount of the policy—and the type."

"Type?" Duncan repeated. "Since when are you such an expert on insurance?"

"I retain a lot of trivia that I read," she told him with a careless shrug.

"You mean like a photographic memory?" he asked, surprised.

"Something like that." Her tone was dismissive. She didn't want him making a big deal of it. But the truth of it was that she remembered practically everything she read or experienced.

"Give me a sec," Valri said. There was a burst of keys being pressed, and then she looked up. "He was born October 7, 1930." She proceeded to rattle off Walt's social security number and concluded with the face amount of the policy as well as the type of policy that had been issued. "It was a ten-year term life insurance policy for a hundred thousand dollars and it was issued a little more than two years ago." Valri looked up, slightly puzzled. "A hundred thousand is a lot, but is that enough to kill for?"

"It is if you don't have it," Noelle pointed out. "Where's the company's home office?"

Valri held up her index finger as she scrolled down the virtual page. "Dearborn, Michigan," she said, reading the address.

Duncan sincerely doubted that Walt would have flown to Dearborn to sign the papers. "How about a satellite office?" he asked.

Valri went to the page that delineated the location of several nearby offices with the aid of a zip code. "Got it! They've got one in Shady Canyon," she read, then rocked back in her chair. "Wow, small world, huh, Duncan?" she observed, glancing toward her brother. For them, as well as the newly discovered branch of the family, Shady Canyon was home.

"Give me the address," Duncan requested.

Writing it down on a half-used pad she found in the corner of Anderson's desk, Valri handed the address to him.

The address that Valri had uncovered brought them to a five-story building that was partially gutted by fire. It was also scheduled to be demolished later that month.

"Well, if there ever *was* a satellite office here, it's gone now," Noelle declared, clearly frustrated by this latest dead end. "I'm beginning to feel like we're just chasing our tails," she complained as they walked back to Duncan's vehicle.

"Not that the image isn't an intriguing one," Duncan commented, glancing at what he had already discovered for himself was her very shapely posterior, "but there has to be some lead we can follow. Whoever is behind all this can't be some criminal mastermind like they portray in the movies. Most criminals tend to be on the dumb side, which means that he or she will slip up, most likely sooner than later."

"Maybe this criminal didn't read the criminal handbook," she quipped drily.

The law of averages was on their side, Duncan silently insisted. "Even if they didn't, he or she is going to make a mistake."

"We can only hope," Noelle said with a sigh as she got back into the car. "Meanwhile, I get to tell Lucy she was right. Not that that's going to make her feel very happy," she predicted. "I'm sure this will be one time that she's going to wish that she was wrong."

"Yeah, but if it wasn't for your grandmother, you wouldn't have ultimately stumbled across this insurance scam," Duncan reminded her. "At least Lucy can take some comfort in that."

"You have a point," she agreed as Duncan pulled away from the curb. "But at her age, it's hard to lose friends."

What his partner said wasn't totally accurate in his opinion. "It's hard to lose friends at any age, but Lucy strikes me as the type who always picks herself up again, and right now, I get the impression that Shamus would like to give your grandmother a hand up to get her back on her feet."

Seeing an opening to make better time, Duncan shifted lanes and merged to the left.

"I've only met the man a few times myself but that last time, at Brennan's wedding, I *know* I saw a definite gleam in his eye when he was talking to Lucy." He slanted a grin in her direction. "You know that old adage about when one door closes, a window opens."

She laughed to herself. "You might have a point there. Windows are always opening for Lucy," she said.

Still, telling her grandmother that someone had murdered her childhood friend was *not* going to be a piece of cake.

By the end of the day, Valri was still trying to untangle the labyrinth that engulfed not just one foundation but all four of them. Each had a different network of holding companies obscuring any clear picture of the foundation and its goals as well as its founders and prominent donors.

The uniformed officer was literally focused on nothing else except the ever-changing screen of her borrowed laptop.

Coming up behind her, Noelle laid a hand on the younger woman's shoulder. Valri nearly jumped.

That convinced Noelle even more that this woman needed some rest.

"Valri, go home," Noelle urged. "Tomorrow's another day, maybe you'll have better luck in the morning."

"C'mon, kid," Duncan said, adding his voice to his partner's, "it's time to pack up your stubborn streak and go home. We need you sharp. Punchy, you're not any good to us."

Valri didn't even look up. "I just need another half hour."

"And you'll have it," Duncan promised, then added, "Tomorrow."

Valri opened her mouth to argue, but then seemed

to reconsider. "Okay," Valri agreed. "See you in the morning." With that, she powered down the laptop, waited until the screen went black and then picked up the shoulder bag she'd brought with her when Duncan had escorted her up here.

Noelle remained in the room until she was satisfied that Valri was really leaving the squad room and going home.

When his sister finally walked out, Noelle looked at her partner. "You're very forceful with your sister."

He wasn't sure if that was admiration in Noelle's voice or surprise. His answer would have been the same either way.

"Valri knows I can take her," he said with a laugh. Duncan followed her out of the squad room and to the elevator. "You want to grab something to eat?" he suggested.

"I think I'm actually too tired to chew," she told him, shaking her head. "Besides, I still have to tell Lucy she was right about Henry's death." And though it provided a kind of closure for her grandmother, she was still dreading having to say the words to her.

"Need some backup?" he asked. The elevator car that arrived was filled to capacity. He waved it on.

Noelle was about to turn down his offer, then thought better of it. "Yes, that would be very nice of you."

The next elevator car was empty. They got on. "I live to please."

Noelle smiled. "I think you covered that pretty well last night."

Duncan grinned, but for once, said nothing. He didn't have to.

Chapter 17

"I was right, wasn't I?" Lucy said the moment Noelle and Duncan walked in. It was more of an assertion than a question. "Henry didn't die of natural causes or because he was seventy-nine, did he?" Noelle's grandmother looked from her to Duncan, no doubt growing certain by the moment. "He died because someone killed him and made it look as if he'd died in his sleep." The woman closed her eyes and shook her head. "I *knew* it."

"Lucy, I haven't said anything yet," Noelle protested. She'd wanted to somehow soften the blow for her grandmother, not just have the fact blurted out like some player shouting "Bingo!" at a weekly game.

"You don't have to," Lucy told her as the woman

crossed to them in the living room. "It's right there, all over your face. Don't ever play poker, kid. They'll clean you out within the first couple of hands," Lucy warned. And then she turned to look at Duncan. "So what are you going to do to catch this SOB who did away with my friend?"

"First we have to figure out who the SOB is," Duncan replied.

He felt for the woman. Beneath the bravado he could detect a layer of pain. He'd seen it countless times before, the frustration felt by the family and friends of a victim, forced to stand on the sidelines, wanting to do something and feeling absolutely help- less at the same time.

Lucy frowned, as if the answer was obvious and right in front of them. "Well, since nobody at the home had a beef with him, my guess would be who- ever was on the receiving end of that stupid life in- surance policy he had."

Leaving her shoulder bag on the coffee table, Noelle removed her service weapon as well as her backup piece and placed it inside of a small lockbox on the top shelf of the coat closet. "Lucy, what do you know about the foundation Henry left his money to?" she asked.

"Nothing," Lucy said flatly. "He never told me about the organization, although I *know* that Amanda woman must have had something to do with it," she insisted, referring to the volunteer she'd locked horns with the morning Henry was found dead. "But even if it's legitimate, charities have been known to have embezzlers in their organization. Maybe someone needed money to get them out of a jam and saw a way to make a quick buck by getting the life insurance money."

Avoiding Duncan's eyes, Noelle felt she needed to rein in her grandmother's suspicions, at least for now, even though she'd already voiced the idea to Duncan earlier. She didn't want Lucy working herself up until they had some concrete proof.

"That's a little far-fetched, Lucy."

"Is it?" Lucy countered. "Henry's dead, isn't he? And someone made him that way. Without an enemy to point to, the insurance money is the first thing that pops up. I don't think a foundation would look to get rid of him, but a person, well, that's another story."

"Your grandmother's one sharp lady, O'Banyon," Duncan commented.

Lucy beamed at him and for one moment, the sorrow left her eyes. Noelle blessed him for that.

"Thanks, handsome," Lucy said. "So, what are you and Noelle going to do about it? If it were me, I'd march right up to that foundation and demand to start looking at their books. Maybe the insurance money wasn't even sent to them. Maybe it was detoured," Lucy said, the idea coming to her as she spoke.

"Not as easy as it sounds," Noelle said, trying to curb her grandmother's imagination before it ran off with her.

"Why?" Lucy challenged, her hands on her hips. For a little woman, she was formidable.

"Because we're not sure just where this foundation is located or who actually runs it. Finding that out is going to take more digging," she told the older woman. "It appears that there are a number of holding companies involved."

Lucy frowned, doing her best to cut through and simplify the rhetoric. "What are they holding?" Lucy asked.

"The truth, hostage, apparently," Noelle answered.

Duncan took Lucy's hands in his, instantly commanding her attention. "We'll get to the bottom of this, Lucy," he promised the woman. "You have my word on that."

Until this moment, she had thought of her grandmother as a sort of iron butterfly. But she could see that Lucy never stood a chance against Duncan. The man wielded charm as if it was a sharply honed sword.

"Good enough for me," Lucy finally responded when she regained her composure. So saying, she then slanted a glance at her granddaughter. "You found a good one, kid."

"I didn't 'find' him, Lucy. Cavanaugh was thrust on me by Lieutenant Jamieson six months ago," she clarified.

"Doesn't matter how it happened, just matters that it did," Lucy told her with an enigmatic smile. "Okay, unless you two want me hanging around babysitting Melinda in case she wakes up, I'm going to be heading home." She looked from her granddaughter to Duncan, waiting for either to tell her to remain. "Going, going, gone," she declared, doing a countdown like an auctioneer.

Lucy crossed to the front door. "Okay, I'll see you in the morning."

Pausing there for one last wave, the next moment Lucy was gone.

Duncan glanced at his wristwatch. "Well, I'd better hit the road, too," Duncan said. "Unless..." he began, his eyes meeting hers.

She knew it was better for both of them if she'd just agree to his departure plans and walk him to the door. The last thing she wanted was further entanglements. As it was, it was going to take her a while before last night did not spring up in her mind like the proverbial gangbusters.

However, her brain seemed determined to play devil's advocate and she gravitated to the word that was hanging in the air between them.

"Unless?"

"Unless you'd like me to hang around for a while," Duncan offered, then completed his thought. "You know, for company."

Tell him that's okay. Tell him you're fine and don't need any company. For heaven's sake, tell him to go!

None of her thoughts made it to her lips. Instead, Noelle smiled at him in response and said, "That would be very nice."

Turning on her heel, she made her way to the family room and sat down on the sofa. Duncan followed and took a seat beside her. He slipped his arm around her shoulders and drew her to him in a movement so fluid, so natural, it was as if they'd been like this for years.

Duncan heard her laughing softly to herself. "What?" he asked, curious.

Shifting her head on his shoulder, she looked up at him, doing her best to ignore the little somersault her heart executed. "When I first came on the job, you were this hot bachelor—"

"Still am," he deadpanned.

"Granted," she allowed with an amused smile. "But back then, it seemed like you had a hot date waiting for you almost every night and I had the impression that outside of the job, all you did was party. *Constantly.* I used to wonder how you kept going."

"Vitamins," he quipped, and then added in a voice that was slightly more serious, "And it wasn't quite every night."

"Certainly seemed that way to me," she answered. "Especially if I went according to what you said."

"I might have exaggerated a little," he conceded, his mouth curving at the corners. "After all, I had a reputation to maintain."

She laughed shortly at the mention of his so-called "reputation." "I thought you were this insufferable egotist. It took me a while to realize you weren't a half-bad detective."

"Half-bad?" he echoed, sounding as if he was taking offense.

Had she insulted him? She hadn't meant to, especially not when he'd been incredibly thoughtful toward her grandmother as well as toward her.

"*Weren't* half-bad," Noelle emphasized. "Actually, you turned out to be pretty good," she amended.

Duncan cocked his head, pretending to think over her revised sentence. "Better," he allowed, "but not there yet."

She shifted against him so that her mouth was closer to his as she asked, "And just what would bring me 'there'?"

"We'll have to work on that," Duncan said as he gave in to the moment and the woman.

Brushing his lips against hers, he waited for Noelle to pull back, or murmur that she was too tired, or just give him a look that would tell him there would be no repeat of last night, at least not tonight. He made it a point to never take *anything* for granted when it came to a woman. Just because they had made love one night did not automatically mean that lovemaking fell under the category of business as usual. *Or* that a repeat performance was even in the offing.

Much as he caught himself wanting her, wanting her even more than the first time if that was possible, he was willing to give her space if she needed it.

As tempting as her lips had just been, he held off kissing her again.

And waited, mentally crossing his fingers and, for a second, holding his breath.

But space wasn't what she wanted. *He* was what she wanted and she made that clear to him in no uncertain terms when she kissed *him,* putting her heart and soul into the simple contact.

She'd very easily stolen his breath away and heated his body in one quick swoop.

"I thought you said you were too tired to chew," he reminded her with a laugh.

"I'm not chewing," she pointed out tantalizingly, teasingly, brushing her lips against his.

"No," he agreed just before his lips covered hers again possessively, "you're not."

If he had any other plans for the evening, they obligingly, immediately went up in smoke.

"I'm going to have to stop by my place and change before I start to smell gamey," he told Noelle after he'd taken a quick shower in her bathroom the following morning.

Mindful of her daughter waking up at any moment, Noelle had already showered and was dressed, ready to face any scrutiny that might come up from the six-year-old.

Unable to force herself to look away, she watched as Duncan quickly pulled his clothes on. Each time she saw his body like that, it was even better than the last time. An impossibility by all accounts—except that it was true.

"Your clothes smell fine," she finally said, then reminded him, "You weren't in them when you were at your most active. But someone's bound to notice that you haven't changed them in three days so maybe you'd better get some fresh ones."

"The squad's filled with guys. They wouldn't notice if I came in wearing a toga. Valri, however, would," he said, "and I really don't want to go through that." He paused to give Noelle a quick kiss before he headed for the door.

He opened it just as Lucy was about to use her key. Far from appearing startled, Noelle's grandmother gave him a once-over as if she was expecting to find him just where he was. "You might want to think about leaving a change of clothes here," she suggested, breezing into the living room.

Duncan mumbled something unintelligible under his breath about women and their powers of observation as he left.

"I didn't scare him away, did I?" Lucy asked as she passed her granddaughter and made her way into the kitchen. Once there, she deposited her oversize purse on the island in the middle of the room.

"You didn't scare anyone away, Lucy. Cavanaugh comes and goes on his own terms," Noelle murmured, only half listening.

She'd taken out her phone to check how much battery she had left—she'd failed to charge it the night before. The first thing to pop up was the photograph she'd been looking at last night—the sketch that had been created from Johnson's description of the woman who'd had such an overwhelming effect on his neighbor.

There was still something oddly familiar about the sketch, and yet she couldn't put her finger on it. Probably because it reminded her of dozens of other sketches she'd seen before, Noelle told herself. With a sigh, she put down her cell and got back to the business of getting ready to leave.

"I heard Melinda stirring. She's probably almost ready, Lucy. I'm running a little behind today. Would you mind getting her breakfast for her before you take her to school?"

Lucy flashed a wide smile. "No problem. I love being needed," she said. "Without Henry to visit at the home, I'll have more time to spend with Melinda—and maybe even see you once in a while," she concluded with a deliberate bright smile.

"Very funny." Noelle crossed to the hall closet and took down the lockbox. Unlocking it, she removed her weapons and armed herself. "What's this I hear about you and Shamus Cavanaugh?"

"A lady never kisses and tells," Lucy maintained with a toss of her head.

Noelle hurried back to the kitchen, her eyes wide with surprise. "You've been kissing Shamus?"

Lucy gave her an utterly innocent look. "What part of 'never kisses and tells' don't you understand?"

Lucy was pulling her leg—or maybe not. With her grandmother, it was hard to tell if she was serious or just having fun teasing her. Resigning herself to knowing the truth of the matter when Lucy was good and ready to tell her, Noelle just shook her head as she left the room.

When she returned five minutes later with a mostly sleepy-eyed Melinda, Lucy had a rather perplexed expression on her face. "What's up?" Noelle asked her.

Her grandmother held up the cell phone that she had left on the island and asked, "What are you doing with a likeness of that awful woman on your phone?" Lucy's frown deepened as she regarded the sketch again.

"Awful woman?" Noelle repeated, confused for exactly ten seconds before she realized who Lucy was referring to. "Sit down, Melinda, Lucy's getting your breakfast ready." Noelle turned to her grandmother and asked in a stunned voice, "You *know* her?"

"Of course I know her. And you met her," she said in a voice that was just a shade away from being accusatory. "She was at the funeral. Amanda. I *told* you about her. She was that horrible woman who volunteered at Henry's assisted living facility. She tried to make me go away that last morning I came to visit him. The woman had the gall to tell me to leave because Henry was sleeping and didn't like being disturbed." Lucy snorted. "Like that hussy knew him and *I* didn't."

Noelle's heartbeat went up a notch. Even so, she told herself not to get excited. Not yet.

"You're sure that it's her?" she asked, taking the cell phone and turning it around so that Lucy was forced to take a closer look at the likeness.

"Of course I am," she said emphatically, pushing the phone away. "You saw her," Lucy repeated. "She was the only other woman who showed up at Henry's funeral." Even the very memory had Lucy scowling.

That was why the woman in the sketch had looked so naggingly familiar to her. She realized that she'd been too caught up in her grandmother's distress to focus on the other woman at the time, only noticing the stranger peripherally.

"You still haven't told me why you're carrying around that sketch of her. Is she launching a campaign to become your new best friend, like she tried to do with Henry?" Lucy asked sarcastically.

"No, Lucy," Noelle said. Could it really be this simple? Had the answer been staring her in the face all along? It didn't really seem possible. "This is the sketch our artist came up with when a witness described the woman who had talked his friend into getting a life insurance policy." She looked at her grandmother as she emphasized, "His *dead* friend."

"I knew it," Lucy cried in a voice so loud, Melinda stopped trying to drown the little circles in her cereal bowl and looked alert for the first time. Lucy stepped away, lowering her voice as she continued. "I knew she had something to do with all this. Well, what are you waiting for?" she asked. "Go and arrest the hussy."

"Momma, what's a *hussy?*" Melinda piped up.

"A lady Lucy doesn't like, sweetie. Finish your cereal, you've got to get going," Noelle told her daughter. Turning her attention back to her grandmother, she motioned Lucy away from the table, turned her back to her daughter and lowered her voice as she told Lucy. "First we'll have to bring this Amanda in for questioning."

"So go, question," Lucy ordered, waving her granddaughter to the front door. "She's probably at the seniors' home, waiting to kill someone else for their policy."

"What's her last name?" Noelle asked. Although, given that each of the other two people she'd talked to had referred to the woman involved by a different first name, she doubted if the surname was going to be her real last name—but there was always that chance.

"She said it was Wright. *W-R-I-G-H-T.* Amanda Wright," Lucy told her.

"Did she ever go by *Susan* or *Virginia?*" Noelle asked her grandmother.

Suspicion instantly clouded Lucy's face. "Why? Are those her aliases?"

"Well, it's certainly beginning to look that way," Noelle replied. Doubling back to the kitchen, she kissed Melinda on the forehead. Both her little girl and her grandmother were her anchors. They were why she could do the job in the first place.

"Have a good day, pumpkin," she murmured to her daughter. "You, too, Lucy," she added for good measure before she quickly made her way out the door and down to her driveway.

Noelle waited until after she had started the car and pulled away from her house before taking out her cell and calling her partner. With each ring on the other end of the cell, her agitation mounted.

"Pick up, pick up!" she urged. "You have me go to voice mail and you're going to regret it, Cavanaugh," she threatened.

Duncan came on the line just in time to hear her issue the warning.

"What are you going to do, O'Banyon? Spank me? Or is your idea of punishment to send me to bed by myself?" he asked, amused.

She was *not* going to rise to that bait, Noelle swore silently. Out loud she informed him, "I think we just caught a break."

"Is that personally or professionally?"

Now what was *that* supposed to mean? Noelle couldn't help wondering. "I'm talking about the case, Cavanaugh, the case."

"I'm listening," he said, his voice serious.

"Lucy recognized the woman in that sketch we had drawn. It's the same woman who turned up at Henry's funeral. I think you caught a glimpse of her."

"Can't be the same one," he told her.

"Okay, I'm listening," she said, flying through a yellow light. "Why can't it be the same one?"

"Because according to Johnson, the woman had a huge chest. The woman at the funeral was average at best."

"You checked her out?" Noelle cried.

"I noticed the total person. It's my job to be observant," he explained.

"Yeah, right." He was all male. But then, she already knew that and his excuse did have validity to it. "Well, her measurements could have easily been enhanced in order to 'mesmerize' her prey. I still think this is worth checking out."

"No argument," he agreed.

"According to Lucy, this woman was very possessive of Henry. Most likely, she talked Henry into getting that life insurance policy."

"Does Lucy know her name?" Duncan asked.

"Yes, but it's probably an alias, like the others. So far, if she's our suspect, she's gone by three different names."

"Three," he repeated. "And who knows how many we haven't gotten wind of yet," Duncan wondered out loud. "This could be bigger than we thought—than you thought," he said, giving her credit for stumbling across the plot in the first place.

"I want to bring her in for questioning," she told Duncan. "According to Lucy, the woman volunteers at the Happy Senior Retirement Home. With any luck, we can pick her up over there."

"We can check it out," Duncan agreed skeptically. "But what do you want to bet that our volunteer saint has suddenly realized that there might be others who need her services more than the good folks at the seniors' home and she's gone hightailing it to somewhere where she'll hold up until the heat's off."

"I'll pass on that, thanks," she said.

"Why?"

"Because I never bet against a sure thing," she replied, frustrated because she knew that Duncan was right. More than likely, Amanda-Susan-Virginia had cleared out.

Nonetheless, within five minutes of her arrival at the precinct, she and Duncan were on their way to the seniors' home—just in case.

Chapter 18

"Amanda?" Jenny Matthews, the director of the seniors' retirement home where Lucy's friend had resided looked genuinely unhappy at the mention of the volunteer's name. "Wonderful woman," the tall, slightly over-made-up woman said mournfully. "So good with the residents. I'm afraid we've lost her."

Noelle exchanged glances with her partner. "As in dead?" she asked the director.

"Dead?" Jenny echoed, stunned. "Oh, no, no, as in she told us that she regrettably wouldn't be volunteering here any longer. It happened right after Henry passed on. My guess is that the mortality rate here finally got to her." The woman paused to sign a requisition order an administrative assistant brought to her. "It is difficult," the director continued, "building relationships with the guests and then suddenly, just like that, they're not there anymore."

"Especially if she helps them along on their way," Noelle murmured under her breath.

The director turned toward her, a slightly puzzled expression on her face. "I'm sorry, I'm afraid I didn't catch that."

"I said it must be difficult seeing them go that way," Noelle told her, quick to cover her unconscious slip. "Would you happen to know if she accepted another position?"

Jenny shook her head. "Sorry, I have no way of knowing that. We didn't pay her here, so it's not like she left for a better paying job." The director paused to think for a moment. "She might be volunteering somewhere else in a different type of facility," Jenny suggested. "I did once hear her mention that she was really interested in helping the homeless. You might try looking for her at one of the local shelters," the woman suggested. And then curiosity got the better of her. "If you don't mind my asking, why are you looking for Amanda?"

Noelle fell back on an old standard excuse rather than tell the woman that they weren't at liberty to say. The latter always sent up red flags and if the director *was* possibly still in touch with the woman they were looking for, she might warn her.

"We think she might have been a witness to a car

accident so we'd like to ask her a few questions about it," Noelle told the other woman.

"Would you happen to have her address on file?" Duncan asked. He didn't hold out much hope of a positive answer, given the director's laid-back attitude, but it certainly wouldn't hurt to ask.

"As a matter of fact, I do." She opened a large bottom drawer and began going through a haphazard pile of files. "I have everyone—employees *and* volunteers—fill out their pertinent information, especially where they can be reached in case of an emergency." Discarded files were carelessly dropped on the floor. "You never know when that can come in handy. Ah, here she is," Jenny declared, plucking a single eight-by-ten sheet of paper and holding it aloft. "Let me just make a copy of that for you," she said, turning her chair to the side where a combination scanner, printer and fax machine resided. "You police certainly are thorough, following up on car accidents like this."

"Protect and serve, that's us, ma'am," Duncan said. He accepted the copy that the director handed him and rose from his seat. "Thank you for your time."

If the director had beamed any harder, her face might have cracked. "My pleasure, Detective."

"I think she just purred," Noelle observed under her breath as they walked out of the woman's office. The front door was only a few feet away. "You do have a power over women."

"Strictly your imagination," he responded.

It wasn't until they'd left the building and were at his car that he took time to look at the page in his hand. When he did, he frowned.

Alarms instantly went off in Noelle's head. "What is it?"

"Well, unless Amanda-Susan-Virginia is part dolphin, she can't live here," Duncan told her.

"What d'you mean?"

He crumpled up the sheet the director had given him. More likely than not, everything else on the page was a lie, as well. "The address puts her smack in the middle of the San Francisco Bay."

Noelle squelched the impulse to take the paper from him and look for herself. She knew he'd take it as an insult. She would have in his place. Still, she had to ask him, "You're sure?"

Duncan got into his car, far from happy. "Geography isn't my specialty, but yeah, I'm sure."

Noelle got in on her side and reached for her seat belt. "Now what?"

He had only one option at the moment. "We go back to the precinct and hope that Valri's found something we can work with."

Valri was seated where she had been placed the day before, diligently working when they came into the squad room. She must have been so absorbed in what she was doing that she didn't even notice them approaching until Duncan and Noelle were practically on top of her.

Valri glanced up at Duncan, a smug smile curving her lips. "Tell me I'm your favorite sister," she told him.

"You're my favorite sister," he parroted, then asked, "Okay, what's my prize?"

But Valri shook her head. She was still typing, verifying something. "Not finished yet." She continued laying down her terms. "And if you feel the need to criticize me or any of the guys I go out with—you'll keep your mouth shut."

A slight edge of impatience entered his voice. "It'll be hard, but okay."

"And—"

That was when he cut his sister short. "I'm not a genie granting three wishes here, Val. Now, what did you find?" he asked.

"Each one of the four charity foundations turned out to be bogus," she announced with finality.

"What about the holding companies? You said you found that there were holding companies involved," Noelle protested.

"Turns out that they were just empty shells," Valri replied. "I went round and round, following every trail, every lead." She laughed shortly. "The holding companies turn out to be just holding each other. I finally managed to track each foundation down to a post office box. The *same* post office box," she underscored significantly, looking from her brother to

Noelle. She picked up the piece of paper where she'd jotted down the number of the PO box as well as the address where it could be located. "This is it."

Taking the paper from her, Duncan memorized the address, then gave Valri a quick, heartfelt squeeze and declared, "You're the best, Valri."

"We've already established that," Valri replied happily. "And she's my witness," she added, nodding at Noelle.

"Absolutely," Noelle confirmed. Then, looking at Duncan, she said, "Let's get down there before Amanda-Susan-Virginia picks up her last piece of 'mail' and clears out."

"Who?" Valri asked, confused.

"Inside joke. I'll explain everything later," Noelle promised. "But right now, we might be fighting a clock." Actually, she was rather certain that they were. The woman was cutting her ties, leaving her familiar stomping grounds. That meant she was either getting ready to set up a new operation—or she was leaving the area altogether and calling it quits.

Noelle rather doubted it was the latter. Once a thief, always a thief. But she had a gut feeling that their window of opportunity was about to close—if it hadn't already.

They were back in the car in another ten minutes. Valri had sent Duncan a text earlier that Woodland Life had received all the necessary documentation and had processed Henry's life insurance policy. The check had been cut and made out to the charitable foundation the man had designated. It had been mailed out yesterday.

That meant it was on its way to the post office box. With any luck, their suspect was going there to pick it up.

Bending a few speed limits, they arrived at the address that Valri had given them and quickly verified that the box was indeed in use, having been rented out to a Curtis Abernathy over a year ago.

"Who the hell is Curtis Abernathy?" Noelle wondered out loud when they got back into Duncan's car, now parked across the street from the post office.

"Beats me," Duncan responded. Traffic was whizzing by in both directions, at times obscuring his view of the building's door.

"I think maybe we've stumbled across a ring, Cavanaugh," Noelle theorized, quickly coming to the conclusion that there was no long-term comfortable position to be found sitting in a car. Surveillance promised to be an endurance test of both her patience and her posterior.

Instead of commenting directly on what she'd just said, Duncan surprised her by saying, "We make a pretty good team."

She stopped shifting and let the words sink in. And then she smiled. "I guess we do. I had my doubts about us in the beginning," she admitted, "but we seemed to have hit our stride."

"Speaking of which, what do you think about marriage?"

Where had that come from? Stunned, she stared at Duncan, but there was nothing in his expression to tell her where he was going with this.

The inside of her mouth felt rather dry as she asked, "As an institution, in general, or—?"

Noelle didn't get a chance to finish. "To me," Duncan told her. "Marriage to me."

She took a breath and pretended they were just having a philosophical conversation. That he didn't mean anything by his question and this was just a way to while away the time. "I think whoever winds up marrying you is in for one hell of a ride."

Duncan blew out an impatient breath. He should have known asking her wasn't going to be a walk in the park. The woman was nothing if not complicated.

"You want me to spell it out, don't you?" he asked her. "Okay, I'm spelling it out—will you marry me?"

Though she'd gone numb, she was pretty sure that her jaw had dropped. "You're serious?" It was half question, half stunned statement.

"Yes," he replied firmly. "I am."

She had to be hallucinating—or just dreaming. There was no other explanation for this. "You're actually asking me to marry you?" she asked incredulously.

"Yes," he answered a little less patiently than before.

This had to be a joke, or a test, right? "In the middle of a stakeout?" she cried.

"No, not in the middle of a stakeout. We'll have

a few dates, see how that goes—and then we'll get married," Duncan told her. "Look, I've seen you under fire, I've seen how you operate, the way you can think on your feet—and most of all, I've seen you with your family and with mine. We've got the same values, and no other woman has even come close to making me want to have something permanent. But you do. So, what do you think?" he asked hopefully.

As far as he was concerned, the conditions were right and he wanted to act on them before something happened to change the playing field. He was aware that Noelle had baggage that caused her to be spooked easily when it came to commitment—and prior to now, *he* had never even entertained the idea of commitment, but it was as if everything had suddenly aligned itself in his head and now this was *all* he wanted.

Noelle stared at him. "Are you out of your mind?"

"That wasn't quite the answer I was hoping for, but no, not since I last checked."

"No," Noelle answered with feeling, remembering what had happened to her last two fiancés. Maybe she was being overly superstitious, but she couldn't help it. Not after having to go through the ordeal twice.

Duncan's eyes held hers, pinning her in place. "You're turning me down?"

"Yes." It was the hardest word she had ever had to utter.

Duncan grabbed on to the word as a response to his proposal. "You're *not* turning me down?" he asked somewhat uncertainly.

"This is for your own good," she began to tell him, then stopped as she saw the object of their surveillance getting out of her car. The woman was heading straight for the post office. "Three o'clock," Noelle exclaimed.

Duncan blinked, trying to make sense of what she was saying. "You want to skip the dating and get married at three o'clock? Fine by me."

"No! Damn it, Duncan, get your mind on the case," she cried, physically turning his head toward the post office. "Our quarry is at three o'clock. Or more like one o'clock now," she amended.

Duncan focused to see the woman Johnson had wistfully described and Lucy had identified walking into the post office. He was out of the car the moment she disappeared into the building. They had previously verified that there was only one exit out of the post office that was accessible to the customers, which meant that their suspect had to come out the exact same way that she'd gone in.

Fifteen minutes after she had entered the building, the woman they thought of as Amanda exited, looking very pleased with herself.

"Amanda Wright?" Noelle asked, falling into step with the former seniors' home volunteer as she flanked the woman's right side.

The woman flashed an appropriate blank expression. "I'm afraid you have me mixed up with some-one else," she said.

"Susan?" Duncan asked as he closed in on the woman's left side.

"I'm sorry, that's not my name, either," the woman replied, keeping her eyes straight ahead of her as she quickened her pace.

"How about Virginia?" Noelle asked. "Does that ring a bell?"

"No," the woman snapped, then struggled to get herself under control as she continued walking quickly to her car. "Should it?"

"Apparently not," Duncan said philosophically.

"Well, what's in a name anyway?" Noelle shrugged dismissively. "As far as I'm concerned, you can call yourself Strawberry Delight, it really doesn't matter. You're still going down for the murder of Henry Robbins, Walter Teasdale, Sally Fowler and Alfie Brown. Probably more. Any other names will be added to the list as we uncover them," she promised the other woman.

"Amanda Wright" stopped walking and glared at her. "I have no idea what you're talking about."

"Then we'll explain to you on the way down to the precinct," Noelle said, taking a firm hold of the woman's arm. "Oh, and before I forget," she plucked the letter that Amanda had in her hand, "we'll be re-lieving you of that envelope you're holding."

"You can't take that. That belongs to the foundation," the woman cried indignantly. "I'm just picking it up to take over to them."

"Sure you are," Duncan said with just a touch of sarcasm in his voice. Glancing down at the envelope to verify the sender—Woodland Life—he began to read the woman her Miranda rights, raising his voice progressively louder to be heard above the barrage of expletives she was hurling at both of them.

In the end, in response to a plea bargain that took the death penalty off the table in exchange for life in prison without the hope of parole, Alice Barnes, aka Amanda Wright, Susan Abernathy, Virginia Sommers and a host of other aliases, gave them the names of her two accomplices. One was an insurance broker Geraldine Lopez, who agented for all the major insurance companies and was instrumental in getting the policies fast-tracked. The other was a con artist, Willow Collins, who it seemed was responsible for coming up with the original plan. Among other courses of action, pretending to be affiliated with a local charity, Alice and Willow would pick up homeless men, provide them with food, clothing, a hotel room and money in exchange for their signatures on insurance polices.

Initially, they had just held on to the policies until the policy holders died, but greed had them quickly escalating their approach, "helping" the people exit this life more quickly.

"For six months to a year, we gave them a decent

place to stay and we gave them hope, which was a hell of a lot better than anything they had going for them when we found them," Alice told the assistant district attorney taking down her statement.

After it was all over, Noelle was still stunned by both women's callous approach to the string of murders. "I honestly think she has no regrets about what she's done," Noelle said. Closing her eyes, she rocked back in her chair in the squad room and shook her head. "Every time I think I've seen the worst mankind can offer, it gets worse," she sighed.

Duncan came around to her desk and sat down on the edge of it. "Not all the monsters are found in fairy tales and nightmares."

Noelle's laugh had no humor in it. "You've got that right."

"Hell of a job, you two," Jamieson said just as he was leaving for the evening. "Glad you kept at it," he told Noelle. "Just hope this doesn't mean you'll be transferring to Homicide."

At this point, she couldn't think of anything worse than looking at dead bodies for a living. "Nope," she answered the lieutenant with feeling, "you're stuck with us for good."

Jamieson nodded as a hint of a smile faintly curved his mouth. "I'll try to bear up to that." Executing a minor salute, the lieutenant left the squad room.

The room was eerily quiet. Except for a couple of detectives on the far end of the room, the area was empty. The night shift hadn't come in and day shift had left—except for them and two other detectives.

Noelle stretched at her desk. "Guess it's all over except for the shouting."

Duncan looked down at her from his perch. "Not yet," he said.

Had she forgotten about something? "Oh?"

"You still haven't given me an answer," he reminded her.

She knew immediately what he was referring to. "Yes I did. The answer's no," she said.

"What if I won't accept *no* for an answer?"

"Too bad," she said as she got ready to leave, "it's the only answer you're going to get."

He took her hands in his. Noelle tried to pull them away, but he held on. "You have feelings for me," he insisted.

Well, duh, she thought. "Which is exactly why the answer's no."

Duncan shook his head and sighed. "You're not making any sense."

"Yes, I am," she insisted. He knew her story, why was he giving her such a hard time? Why wasn't he running for the hills? "Two people wanted to marry me. I said yes to each of them. Now they're both dead. Can't you understand? I want you to continue breathing. The answer's no," she repeated.

He refused to believe she was serious. "You can't be that superstitious."

Her eyes narrowed so that all she saw was him. "Try me."

He tried to find a way around this curse that had her paralyzed. "They were both your fiancés, right?"

"Right."

"Engagement ring and everything?"

He knew that, knew all the details. What did he hope to accomplish by reviewing everything? "Yes."

"Okay, then we'll just skip that part. No engagement. We'll go directly to getting married," he told her.

His smile was melting her heart despite all her precautions. "A week from Sunday okay with you?"

Where did she even begin? "You are insane!"

He didn't bother to deny it. "Yes, I am. Insane about you." He *had* to make her understand. He didn't want to be single anymore, didn't want to live without her. "I have been with scores of women—"

Pulling her hands free, she held them up in front of her as if to block his words. "Too much information, Cavanaugh."

Duncan just plowed on as if she hadn't said anything. "And I've never felt about any of them the way I feel about you. You make me want to settle down, Noelle. To sit on a sofa and pop popcorn, for God's sake. You make me want *forever,*" he stressed. "I'd always heard that love packs a punch, but I thought it was just some dumb metaphor at best. Well, it's not a metaphor, it's true. I feel like I've been hit with a two-by-four.

"The first time I kissed you—hell, the first time I *saw* you, I knew. Knew it was just a matter of time before I'd be doing this."

She looked at him uncertainly. "'This'?"

"Asking you to marry me," Duncan explained. "Tell me that you don't love me. It's the only way to get rid of me."

Okay, this was for his own good, not hers. "I don't love you."

He didn't go, didn't budge. "I don't believe you."

She was running out of ways to get him to do the sensible thing while he was still breathing. "Okay, then believe this. I don't want to take the risk."

"The risk is mine to take, not yours," he pointed out. "I'll wear a bulletproof vest if that'll make you feel better."

"Think about it," he told her. "Let's just say I believe in this 'curse,' I just have to get to the altar in one piece. After that, after we're pronounced husband and wife, that so-called 'curse' will be lifted. What do you say?"

"You're not going to stop, are you?" she asked, sensing it was futile to keep saying "no," especially when her heart was pleading "yes."

"Not until I get you to agree," he told her truthfully.

Noelle sighed. "Nobody told me how stubborn you Cavanaughs can be."

Duncan grinned, knowing he'd won. "It's actually our best feature."

"*One* of your best features," Noelle corrected just before she gave in to the overwhelming urge to kiss her very persuasive future husband-to-be. "Okay, yes, I'll date you," she teased just before her lips met his.

Duncan had a feeling the rest of his life would be one hell of an adventure.

* * * * *

MILLS & BOON®

Why not subscribe?
Never miss a title and save money too!

Here's what's available to you if you join the
exclusive **Mills & Boon Book Club** today:

Titles up to a month ahead of the shops
▸ *Amazing discounts*
Free P&P
▸ *Earn Bonus Book points that can be redeemed
against other titles and gifts*
▸ *Choose from monthly or pre-paid plans*

Still want more?
Well, if you join today we'll even give you
50% OFF your first parcel!

So visit **www.millsandboon.co.uk/subs**
or call Customer Relations on 020 8288 2888
to be a part of this exclusive Book Club!

MILLS & BOON®

Why shop at millsandboon.co.uk?

Each year, thousands of romance readers find their perfect read at millsandboon.co.uk. That's because we're passionate about bringing you the very best romantic fiction. Here are some of the advantages of shopping at www.millsandboon.co.uk:

* **Get new books first**—you'll be able to buy your favourite books one month before they hit the shops

* **Get exclusive discounts**—you'll also be able to buy our specially created monthly collections, with up to 50% off the RRP

* **Find your favourite authors**—latest news, interviews and new releases for all your favourite authors and series on our website, plus ideas for what to try next

* **Join in**—once you've bought your favourite books, don't forget to register with us to rate, review and join in the discussions

Visit **www.millsandboon.co.uk**
for all this and more today!